"Jump!"

"The wings are completely iced over!"

The doors opened and immediately the wind and pelting ice slashed at them. Bolan shoved the equipment container forward, trying to push it into the opening. Nischal leaned down to help, then stumbled in the gusting winds.

That was all it took for the icy air to snatch her. She rolled toward the opening away from Bolan's outstretched hand.

"We're going down!" the Major yelled. "Get clear! We'll hold it as long as we can!"

Nischal continued the slide and Bolan saw her reach for and miss the chance to grab one of the support struts on the ramp. She spun around again and her chute snagged on a piece of metal sticking up from the very edge of the ramp. He couldn't hear it over the howling wind, but he could imagine the tearing sound it made.

Her eyes met his and he knew there was nothing for it. He jumped, trying to catch her, but by then she'd torn free and begun the long fall to the ground. Bolan glimpsed the ragged remains of her parachute, still hung up on the cargo bay doors, and at the edge of the ramp, their equipment.

Then he, too, was free-falling into the storm.

MACK BOLAN ®
The Executioner

DON PENDLETON'S
THE EXECUTIONER®

PERILOUS CARGO

A GOLD EAGLE BOOK FROM
WORLDWIDE®

TORONTO • NEW YORK • LONDON
AMSTERDAM • PARIS • SYDNEY • HAMBURG
STOCKHOLM • ATHENS • TOKYO • MILAN
MADRID • WARSAW • BUDAPEST • AUCKLAND

Recycling programs
for this product may
not exist in your area.

First edition March 2015

ISBN-13: 978-0-373-64436-0

Special thanks and acknowledgment to
Dylan Garrett for his contribution to this work.

Perilous Cargo

Man's enemies are not demons, but human beings like himself.

—Lao Tzu

Anyone who makes himself an enemy of innocent people is an enemy of mine. And he doesn't have long for this world.

—Mack Bolan

THE
MACK BOLAN
LEGEND

Nothing less than a war could have fashioned the destiny of the man called Mack Bolan. Bolan earned the Executioner title in the jungle hell of Vietnam.

But this soldier also wore another name—Sergeant Mercy. He was so tagged because of the compassion he showed to wounded comrades-in-arms and Vietnamese civilians.

Mack Bolan's second tour of duty ended prematurely when he was given emergency leave to return home and bury his family, victims of the Mob. Then he declared a one-man war against the Mafia.

He confronted the Families head-on from coast to coast, and soon a hope of victory began to appear. But Bolan had broken society's every rule. That same society started gunning for this elusive warrior—to no avail.

So Bolan was offered amnesty to work within the system against terrorism. This time, as an employee of Uncle Sam, Bolan became Colonel John Phoenix. With a command center at Stony Man Farm in Virginia, he and his new allies—Able Team and Phoenix Force—waged relentless war on a new adversary: the KGB.

But when his one true love, April Rose, died at the hands of the Soviet terror machine, Bolan severed all ties with Establishment authority.

Now, after a lengthy lone-wolf struggle and much soul-searching, the Executioner has agreed to enter an "arm's-length" alliance with his government once more, reserving the right to pursue personal missions in his Everlasting War.

Prologue

Not far from the warehouse, he walked silently over the small stone footbridge that crossed the Bagmati River. Farther upstream, temples lined the banks of the waterway the Hindus and Buddhists believed was holy, but the man was not interested in the spiritual potential of the water—only the rippling, gurgling sound that helped hide his movements. The moonless sky ensured there were plenty of shadows, and the late hour left the streets empty and quiet.

Kathmandu was unlike any other city in the world. It was a city of contradictions—wealthy tourists mingled with poor-by-choice monks and hotels catering to the rich found near ancient shrines. Nepal was a strange place, and Kathmandu, a crossroads of religion, money, crime and constantly shifting political powers, was the hub. He liked it, though he was glad that this night would see him on his way home.

With no fear of being seen by late-night tourists in the remote district, he found the stone shrine he'd been seeking, reached inside to find the switch and slid the hidden panel aside. Cobwebs and dirt covered the handle, but he wiggled it back and forth, eventually pulling it free of its lock. Below the shrine, the opening for the staircase came free, revealing a steeply twisting set of stone stairs. He stepped inside and used another mechanism to close the panel behind him.

The man ignored the torch holders and slipped his night-vision monocle into place. The corridor hadn't been used in years and he chuckled to himself. Some secrets were just forgotten, waiting to be exposed. He knew many of them, in cities and countries far and near. In fact, some might say he was a walking, talking secret himself.

The descent ended and a long corridor stretched ahead of him. He knew the hallway extended beneath a small market square, then a fenced parking area and, eventually, the warehouse. People walked over this passage every day, ignorant of its existence. Part of it was caved in, but he faced nothing more difficult than scrambling over a dirt mound. He paused, caught his breath and then climbed another set of stone stairs that ended in a sealed door above his head. This one opened onto the warehouse floor.

The escape tunnel had originally been dug by monks decades before inside a small temple. Later, the temple had been torn down and the warehouse had been built in its place. During the fall of the USSR, some factions within Russia had needed a facility and thus purchased it for their own use.

The man peered at the door, then found the small niche that would, hopefully, open it after all these years of disuse. He needed all of this to work. And it did. The door opened a crack, enough for him to pull himself up and inside a small office in the warehouse itself. So far, he'd triggered no alarms.

He slipped in, then snuck through the open office door and moved along the wall toward an interior sentry, half-asleep at his post. The man pulled a knife out of his boot. His movements were so swift the sentry had no time to shout as the man clasped a hand over his mouth and shoved the tip of the blade into his carotid artery. He lowered the guard to the ground as he grabbed his ID. After edging along the wall to the main entrance, the man swiped the guard's badge along the electronic keypad and watched the lights flash as the bay door began to open.

He sprinted back toward the massive platform truck with the nuclear warhead attached and began to climb into the cab. Shots rang out and ricocheted off the door. He turned, drawing his own weapon, and fired back, knocking the assailant down in one shot. There was no time for playing around.

He got behind the wheel and started the truck. The warehouse doorway was beginning to fill with Russian soldiers, most of them milling around in confusion. He reached out the window and opened fire, scattering the sentries as they looked for cover. He shifted up another gear and drove through the door before they could lower it again.

He didn't bother to head for the gate, just aimed for the nearest section of chain-link fence and tore through it. The bullets bouncing off the truck didn't bother him. As soon as he cleared the facility he checked his mirrors. No one was in pursuit. The man smiled, knowing the chaos he'd caused would keep them busy. He shifted into high gear and headed for the Friendship Highway.

Everything would be different now. It was only a matter of time.

1

As Hal Brognola, the director of the Sensitive Operations Group based at Stony Man Farm, walked down the silent hallway, he knew that whatever was waiting for him in the Situation Room probably wasn't something he wanted to hear. He sighed and stopped in front of the door, where a silent Marine guard waited. Brognola removed his Justice Department ID card, held it up for the Marine's brief inspection, then swiped it through the reader. The Marine opened the door for him, then stepped aside smartly. "Good evening, sir," he said.

"Want to bet?" Brognola growled under his breath.

Stony Man Farm was a covert operations base whose existence was known by a very few and whose director answered directly to the President. Its missions were varied, ranging from domestic anticrime and terrorism to foreign intelligence operations—anything that the United States couldn't officially be seen—or get caught—doing. Brognola had been in charge for a long time, which perhaps explained why he went through so many antacids in a given day and certainly explained why he knew that a call from the White House at two in the morning wasn't good news.

Inside the Situation Room he'd expected to find a large assortment of military brass, but he was startled to see only one man: the President himself. At the moment, his back was to Brognola as he watched some spy satellite footage playing on one of the many video screens in the room. He turned when the door shut.

"Hal," he said, pausing the feed. "Thank you for coming in."

"Of course, Mr. President," he said. The two men shook hands. "What's the situation?"

The President laughed. "You always come straight to the point, Hal. It's one of the reasons I like you."

"You don't call me at this hour if there *isn't* a situation, sir. Usually a bad one."

"True enough, and this one is more precarious than I'd like, Hal, which is why the only people here at the moment are the two of us. If the Joint Chiefs heard about this, we'd have no way to contain it. As it is, I've had to seal everything with 'Presidential Eyes Only,' and anyone else who's seen it has been sent on a long vacation with direct orders to keep their mouths shut."

"That doesn't sound precarious, Mr. President," Brognola said carefully. "That sounds like an end-of-the-world kind of problem."

"The truth is, Hal, we could be looking at a major disaster, but I think—with your help—we might be able to get on top of it." He turned and restarted the video feed at the beginning. "This is a clip from one of our satellites as it passed over Kathmandu about twelve hours ago. Routine surveillance, so the angle isn't very precise. The analyst who saw this come through cleaned it up and damn near wet himself."

Brognola didn't speak but took up a position next to the President and watched the screen. The blurred images solidified, showing a mobile launching platform, complete with a nuclear warhead and rocket, moving away from a large building. Guards were shooting at the vehicle, but it was heavily armored and kept right on going, hitting the road and then disappearing from the frame. The data analyst was clearly on his game because the next sequence showed the truck on a deserted highway, heading away from the city. Then it was lost again.

"Did he do any still image enhancement?" Brognola asked.

The President nodded and typed in the commands, bringing up the slides. The side of the rocket was in shadow, but the markings were unmistakable. They were Russian.

Brognola nodded thoughtfully, then took a seat at the conference table. After the Cold War, the Soviets had either lost or hidden a large number of nuclear weapons, though which one this represented was impossible to say. "I was right, Mr. President," he said. "Precarious was an understatement. Who else knows about this?"

"The director and deputy director of the CIA, the Vice President, and you," he said. "Plus the soon-to-be-vacationing analyst."

Brognola cleared his throat. "Don't let the analyst go anywhere," he advised. "In fact, have him brought in on some pretense. Arrange for him to be held until this is over."

"You're afraid he'll talk?"

"If he hasn't already, yes, I am. Let's find out for sure if he's made any calls or spoken to anyone since his debrief, and hold anyone he's even said good-night to. He knows there's a nuclear missile roaming around in Nepal or Tibet. I'd suggest we take him out of circulation immediately."

The President glanced at his watch. "He's still in with the deputy director, going over it all one more time. Give me a moment." He picked up a phone, dialed, then spoke softly into the receiver. "It's done," he said. "They'll keep him at Langley for the time being."

"Good. Now, who else knows?"

"I already told you, Hal—"

"Excuse me, sir, I mean which countries?"

"Well, we've got to assume the Russians know—it's their damn missile that's been stolen."

"Did we have any indication that they were housing arms in Kathmandu?"

"There were plenty of rumors at the end of the Cold War, of course, but that's all they were at the time—rumors. The intelligence coming out of the former Soviet Republic was terrible. The CIA didn't have anything concrete or we'd have moved on it long ago."

"But the CIA had something?"

"One field agent offered up an *unconfirmed* report, but it was little more than something he'd heard."

"Based on what we're seeing here, I'd say it's been confirmed," Brognola said.

The President stood and paced while Brognola gathered his thoughts.

"Sir, if China finds out…" he started.

"Then any hope we have for Tibet is lost," he finished. "Worse, if that damn nuke gets launched into China…"

"Then we could be looking at World War III."

"Exactly," the President said. "That seems like a pretty good reason to kick you out of bed, wouldn't you agree?"

"No complaints, Mr. President."

"All right, so what do you recommend?" he asked.

"Have we had any contact with the thief? Any ransom or other demands?"

"No, and I think that's more troubling than anything. Someone after money and power we can negotiate with, but a true believer of some kind or another…"

"In Nepal or Tibet?" Brognola asked. "Is there anything happening with the Chinese that might have motivated this from inside either country?"

"Not that we're aware of, but I'll dig a little deeper into that and see if they've managed to keep something from us. We don't know yet what we're dealing with. If the person who stole it has an agenda, then we've got nothing to give them and no room to negotiate. So I'll ask again, Hal—what are your recommendations?"

"We go in fast and quiet. Striker's the best man for this kind of job—hell, he's the only man for this kind of job."

The President nodded. "Fast and quiet it is, then," he said. "Maybe we'll get lucky and we can put a lid on this before we've got every warlord and criminal in the region going after the warhead, let alone China."

"It's possible," Brognola said. "Anything else, sir?"

"I want to add one to your team," the President replied. "An expert on the region and in the field. Two is better than one on this hunt in case something goes wrong."

"Sir, Striker doesn't always work and play well with others. It's just his nature."

"He will this time, Hal," the President said. "And that's not nature—it's an order."

"Yes, sir." Brognola got to his feet.

"Oh, and Hal?"

"Sir?"

"Let's not drop the ball on this one, okay? I'd hate to have to be the first President since Truman to be responsible for a nuclear holocaust." The President was staring at him very intently, his eyes clear and focused.

"You know that Striker has never dropped the ball, sir," Brognola said. "And he won't now."

2

Mack Bolan had been to the National Mall on a number of occasions, but it was almost never to revel in the monuments to the people and values that had built this country, let alone enjoy the park space. Not that he wanted to play the tourist, but he wouldn't mind coming here once or twice for reasons less imperative than the end of the civilized world. Still, when Hal Brognola had called him early that morning and said they needed to meet immediately, he knew from experience that somewhere in the world his skills were needed.

As he approached the bench where Brognola had suggested they meet, he was surprised to see a woman seated next to the big Fed. The sun had only recently come up, and they appeared to be the only people out on the Mall at the moment. The pair was deep in conversation, and Bolan cleared his throat to announce his arrival.

The woman turned around slowly. "Colonel Stone, I presume?" she said, rising to her feet. "I feared we'd be waiting on you all morning." She shook Bolan's hand and then turned back to Brognola. The action offered an alluring glimpse of her slender neck hidden by long, black hair that fell almost to the small of her back. "I was just running out of stories to tell to fill the time."

"I rather doubt that," Bolan said. "Hal."

"Colonel Stone," Brognola said, also rising to stand. "Thank you for coming. Let me introduce you to Alina Nischal. She's vital to the mission we're about to discuss."

"Pleasure," Bolan said.

Brognola handed Bolan a foam cup of coffee. "Let's walk."

As they crossed the Mall in the cool morning air, Brognola filled them in on the situation. "Approximately forty-eight hours ago, a small nuclear missile, an RT-2PM, on a mobile launching platform was stolen from a secret Russian holding facility in Kathmandu, Nepal. Based on satellite images, it appears to be a complete system, ready for service. The last image we picked up tracked it leaving the city and heading north, toward the border with Tibet."

"Is there any chance it's the Russians stealing one of their own weapons?" Bolan asked. "The black market in that part of the world sells pretty much anything and everything."

"We don't think so," Brognola said. "But we can't discount that possibility."

"Do we know who might have access to that base outside of the Russians?" Nischal asked.

"If we did, this mission would be a whole lot simpler," Brognola told her. "It seems likely that there's been plenty of money thrown around to keep this facility off the radar, but as of right now we don't know who has it and what their intent may be."

"So, you want me to go and recover it?" Bolan asked.

"It's a little more politically complicated than that," Brognola replied. "It's crucial, yes, to recover the weapon, but there's more at play than just the danger this rogue weapon represents. If we can get our hands on it before the Russians do, we can prove that they haven't lived up to the treaties we've signed. Which means a lot of concessions from them at the bargaining table, especially in regard to places like North Korea and Pakistan."

"And if the Russians recover it first?" Nischal asked.

"Then they'll have complete deniability and we'll lose our advantage. There are other considerations, too. It's only a matter of time until the Chinese learn something's going on. Depending on how this plays out, they could decide to launch a military action in Tibet. Worse, if that weapon is launched, then we could be looking at the beginning of World War III."

Bolan nodded thoughtfully. "That's an eight-hundred kiloton weapon with a range of over six thousand miles. Whoever stole it could blow a pretty big hole in a lot of places…India, China, the Middle East."

"Great Britain, America," Nischal added. "Not to mention that a weapon like this violates the very sanctity of what many in the area believe. It could divide the region, sending many into prayer and others off to war. This weapon could cause huge upheaval even if it doesn't blow anything up."

"Hal, how do you want to play this?" Bolan asked.

"It's straightforward enough. We're going to send you in fast and quiet. Retake the weapon and deliver it to Delhi, where we'll have a transport waiting to get it to the United States. After, you'll go back and ensure that we've got on-the-ground intelligence on the facility to confirm our claims."

"How are we going in?" Nischal asked.

"We?" Bolan said. "Who said anything about 'we'? I assumed you were here because you had some kind of intelligence on the situation."

"Colonel Stone, Alina is an expert on the region and she speaks all the languages, including the dialects. Both of you will be going." Brognola's voice was firm.

Nischal smirked. "Don't worry, Colonel. I'm field qualified in weapons, hand to hand and tactics."

"All right," Bolan said. "Let's just hope you can live up to your training. Given the danger, I imagine the alternatives to coming up short will be less than pleasant."

"I'll carry my weight," she replied coolly. "And yours, too, if it comes to that."

"It won't," he said, then looked at Brognola. "What kind of insertion are you planning?"

"We've got a B-2 Spirit on ready alert at Andrews. You'll do a HALO jump just over the border in Tibet." He brought up a map of the region on his phone and showed it to them. "This is a pretty desolate area, but there are several warlords operating in the region, according to our latest intel, so watch yourselves."

"What do we have on them?" Bolan asked. "Anything specific?"

"No one passes in or out of that region without at least one of them knowing," Nischal said. "There is *one* operative who knows everything there is to know about the players in that area, though."

"And who might that be?" Bolan asked.

She raised her hand and fanned her fingers in the air, waving them daintily. "Don't worry, Colonel Stone. I'll take care of you."

"Let's see how it goes in the field before we worry about who's taking care of who," Bolan said dryly.

"And on that charming note, I believe I'll go and get ready. I'll meet you at Andrews, Colonel." She turned and added a respectful goodbye to Brognola.

Bolan watched her saunter off and shook his head. Hopefully, she was more than a pretty face and a sharp mind.

"Hal, we didn't cover this, but how do you expect me to get that damn missile—assuming I can find it—from Tibet all the way to India?"

The big Fed shrugged. "My guess is you'll have to drive it."

"Drive it!" Bolan choked. "You're talking about more than five hundred miles, in hostile territory, in what's likely to be lousy weather."

"Don't forget all the mountains and the wind," Brognola said, chuckling. "Just like when you walked to school back in the day."

"Very funny," he said. "I'm serious. You want me to drive it to Delhi?"

"Unless you come up with a better idea once you've got it, that's the only move we've got in this case."

Bolan sighed heavily and started to say something, but Brognola cut him off. "Before you say anything else about Alina, you know that I can't override the President of the United States. He wants her along and he trusts her for some reason."

"Hal, you're sending us into hostile terrain while we try and track down a nuke. I'll spend the whole mission trying to make certain she isn't killed, and that's assuming she survives a HALO jump out of the cargo bay of a stealth bomber in a country not known for its charming weather conditions."

"Don't count her as baggage just yet, Striker. I've read her file, and I think she'll give you a run for your money. She's the real deal and has been working in the field for the CIA for over a decade. She can handle herself."

Bolan wasn't entirely convinced, but the deal was done. There was no point in arguing any further. "Have a nice trip, Striker," Brognola said. "Try to leave something in Nepal standing. The Chinese will know we've been up to something if Mount Everest isn't there next week."

"I'll do my best."

"You always do," he said. "That's why I'm sending you."

3

The city of Yangon, which had been the capital of Myanmar until the early years of the new millennium, was a mix of the old and the new. Temples and shrines in gold and silver and white upheld the glory of years past, while the city center itself contained both colonial and modern buildings—most of which were tied to the government in one way or another. Much of the hidden work of the regional government was still done in this city, rather than the new capital. The media, including television, radio and the internet, were all tightly controlled, and access to technology was expensive. It was an unhappy place in many ways, despite the charming landscape. Tourists came here and saw nothing of how the population was segmented, keeping to their own areas and minding their own affairs, trying not to be noticed by the oppressive government. Citizens sat on the streets, drinking tea praying at the temples or selling tokens to travelers.

Nizar Vitaly despised the city with a true passion.

His mother was Russian, and he never truly felt at home anywhere else.

Like most government buildings in the area, the Russian Consulate was an older colonial brick building, left behind from when the British ruled the nation. And the heat was as oppressive as any ruler had ever been, too, Vitaly thought as he walked into the main entrance. He was a big man, six foot four, and a solid mass of two hundred and twenty pounds, but he moved like a panther—and he knew it. Vitaly was a man completely aware of himself and his own place in the universe.

He passed the main desk and climbed a flight of stairs to the second floor. He followed a short hallway down to the consul's office and managed to contain his surprise when he saw Anisim Grigori, the head of Russian Intelligence, sitting behind the consul's desk. Vitaly closed the door behind him but noted two other ways to get out of the office if this meeting did not go in his favor for some as yet unknown reason. Certainly, he would not be the first operative killed by his own agency. Being aware of one's own place in the universe meant being aware of one's own mortality, first and foremost.

"Vitaly, it's good to see you," Grigori said, rising to his feet. They shook hands formally. "You are missed in Moscow."

"Yes, sir, thank you," he replied. "I am surprised to see you, I admit. What brings you to Myanmar?"

"There is a problem that I would like you to deal with."

Vitaly kept his peace and waited.

"You are aware, I think, of our…interests in Kathmandu?" Grigori raised a bushy eyebrow.

"You know I am, sir. I recommended changes to the facility's security systems months ago, but my report was filed away."

"Yes, I've seen the report and I've seen to it that those who chose to file it rather than share it with the chain of command are seeing their future in a very different light. A very different light, indeed."

"What has happened?" Vitaly asked. "It must be serious to bring you all the way from Moscow."

"Please, sit," Grigori said, gesturing to the nearest chair. "There is no need to be quite so formal."

Vitaly sat, watching the man who had built the new Russian Intelligence of the internet age with interest. He was dangerous, yes, but he could be a very powerful ally. Vitaly had no interest in doing field work for the rest of his life, and Grigori could secure his future—or destroy it—with a few simple words.

"So, as you say, the matter is serious," Grigori continued. "One of the weapons was stolen and taken into Tibet."

"Do we know who the thief is?"

"No, the identity is uncertain. You will retrieve it and remove all trace of the facility's existence."

Vitaly nodded. "It will be done. In fact, we have options here in Myanmar that are suitable for relocation, and the government is very cooperative."

"I will leave all of that in your hands, Vitaly. Just secure the weapon and wipe the Kathmandu facility off the map. Send me your needs by this evening and I will see to it that you have everything you require."

Vitaly considered the situation. "Once I have the weapon, we'll still have a personnel problem in the region. Too many people know about Kathmandu—especially now. That many will never stay silent."

"I am sure you have heard the phrase, 'dead men tell no tales'?"

"Yes, sir."

"Do I need to say more?"

"No, sir."

"And one more thing, Vitaly. I do not hold any doubts that the Americans may be behind this, or possibly the Chinese. I should not have to tell you how delicate this is for our country. We cannot afford to lose our bargaining position now. Make certain that anyone who knows about the weapon or the facility is removed from the equation."

Vitaly smiled. It was the kind of fieldwork he enjoyed most, and it was much better than skulking around Yangon. What was most important was controlling the information Moscow received. After all, the black market paid far better than the government, though he enjoyed the power and income from both sources. "It will be as you command. No witness will be left alive."

Once he arrived at Andrews Field, Bolan changed into tactical clothing, then headed to the hangar where he found Nischal already waiting for him.

She, too, had switched clothing, and he noticed that she'd chosen appropriately for the mission and the terrain. She nodded as he approached. "Good to see you made it on time, Colonel."

Bolan nodded a curt greeting.

"Look, let's clear something up," Nischal said. "The truth is that I don't usually work with anyone else, either, so I'm probably just as prickly about it as you are.

If you think you can't handle it, I'm happy to take the mission on myself."

Bolan allowed himself a smile and a chuckle. "I'm afraid you're stuck with me. We may not like working with others, but when the President gives an order, we follow it. On that much, we can agree. Let's get this show on the road. Wherever that nuclear missile is, it won't find itself."

They carried their gear aboard the *Spirit of Kitty Hawk*. The pilot and mission commander were already in the cockpit. The intercom system pinged on. "Good evening, Colonel Stone, Ms. Nischal. I'm Major Gage, and your pilot is Lt. Colonel Elliot."

"Gentleman, thanks for the lift. We're ready to go whenever you are. Do you have a specific drop zone in mind at this point?"

"No, sir," the major replied. "All I've got is Tibet. I was told that Ms. Nischal would be providing the drop information en route."

Bolan looked a question at her. "I've got the map data uploaded to my smartphone," she said. "I'll shoot it to them once we're in the air."

"Fine," he said. "Major, we're all set. Let's hit it."

"Yes, sir."

The intercom system pinged off and Bolan turned back to Nischal. "It's your map and region, so let's hear what you've got in mind."

She took out her phone and tapped the keys, bringing up a map of Tibet, then zooming in. "Take a look at this," she said. "This is the village of Nyalam—sort of a crossroads village about twenty miles north of the border with Nepal and about sixty miles west of Mount Everest as the crow flies."

"Okay," he said. "Why there?"

"Well, we know the nuke was headed north, and there aren't very many roads. Most are little more than goat paths or dirt tracks that lead to monasteries. There's only one major highway, and anyone who wants to get anywhere has to use it. This isn't exactly the easiest terrain in the world. If you know the area it's easy to disappear, but a truck that size has to go somewhere. And wherever it goes, some*one* will see it."

"So, you're thinking whoever took the weapon had to pass through Nyalam. In other words, we have a place to start looking."

"Exactly," she said. "And if makes you feel better, Nyalam used to be called the Gate of Hell because the old trail was so treacherous. No one is moving fast through there, even on the Friendship Highway."

Bolan studied the map a minute more, then nodded, impressed. "That all sounds fine to me. You obviously know the area."

"Like the back of my hand," she said.

"Here's what I want to know," Bolan said. "Tibet is a whole lot of empty. Even the capital has less than a million people in it, and most of them are too focused on tourists, religion or dealing with China to be worried about stealing a nuke. Where would someone be taking a weapon like that, given how much they would stick out?"

She shook her head. "On that score, I don't know. If they wanted to disappear, they'd get off the highway and use the mountains as cover. There are hundreds of places to hole up—if you can get to them. There's the plateau region, but it's wide-open. Our eyes in the sky would pick them up before we landed. So, that leaves the road or the mountains. As far as who would take it…that's really the bigger question. This isn't a region that's known for trading in weapons, but I suppose that there's a first time for everything."

The jet began to taxi out of the hangar and the major suggested that they get buckled in, which they did. The seats, such as they were, promised a long, uncomfortable flight. Nischal leaned back and shut her eyes. "Let's just hope someone spotted them before they disappeared, or that they're stuck on the highway in some bad weather traffic jam."

"Somehow, I have my doubts," Bolan said, stretching his legs out.

"Oh? Why is that?"

"Because that would mean we'd been incredibly lucky. My missions don't tend to run along those lines. Usually, it's just the opposite."

"Same with mine," she said. "Honestly, I don't know anyone whose missions run perfectly smoothly. They don't usually call people like you and me when things can be handled with a simple stop."

Bolan knew the long flight would only be made longer by worry. Still, he couldn't help but think that anyone willing to steal a nuclear warhead and head into Tibet was either crazy or really smart—and knew exactly what they were doing. That was a serious cause for concern.

4

The flight was scheduled to take about thirteen hours, including the midair refueling. Bolan and Nischal passed the time by double-checking their gear, the map and the very brief intelligence file and, finally, in desperation, by playing mercenary poker. The boredom was palpable enough that when the jet hit a severe pocket of turbulence and the intercom system pinged with a quick warning to strap themselves in, both of them were stunned for a moment before they leaped to their feet and got back into their safety harnesses.

"What's the situation, Major Gage?" Bolan asked.

"We're about an hour away from your drop zone, sir," he said. "But a major storm is brewing over the Himalayan range. We're going to try and climb out of the worst of it."

"All right," Bolan replied. "Keep us informed."

They could feel the jet rocking in the storm as it climbed, closing in on forty-five thousand feet. Still, the winds lashed at them, and the pilot was slaloming from one pocket of turbulence to the next. After a few minutes, the plane leveled out, but the situation didn't noticeably improve.

"Colonel Stone, radar shows this storm blowing up right in our flight path and your drop zone," Major Gage said. "I'm going to recommend you consider aborting the drop."

"I appreciate that, Major, but we don't have a choice," Bolan said. "We're on a clock and can't afford to lose the time." The plane bounced jarringly as he spoke.

"I understand, sir," he said. "We'll do our best. I recommend you go ahead and suit up and move to the cargo bay."

Bolan looked at Nischal. "Have you ever done a HALO jump before?" he asked.

She nodded. "Yes, though I've never attempted one in weather like this."

"It could make it interesting," he admitted. They moved to the cargo area, and Bolan affixed the drop chute to the metal equipment container, which held everything they couldn't carry on their persons— weapons, MREs and tactical communication and observation gear, for the most part.

Nischal was studying the altimeter on the wall. "We're all over the place," she said, bracing herself as the plane dropped suddenly, then came back up. "We should prep as if we were going to jump from forty-thousand feet."

"Let's put on the oxygen masks now, then," Bolan said. "This is no time for either one of us to get hypoxic."

As the plane continued to bump, shudder, rise and fall through the storm, Bolan checked the wall gauges again. At the moment, they were at thirty-two thousand feet.

And dropping.

The plane shuddered all around them, and Bolan keyed the intercom system. "Major, what's going on up there?" he barked.

"We've got facing wind speeds of sixty-plus miles an hour, and we're icing over, sir," he said. "The flaps are…"

Bolan's stomach rolled as the descent became sharper, then leveled slightly. "The flaps are what?" he shouted.

"We've got ice warnings in the wing system. Having trouble maintaining altitude and direction."

"Damn it," Bolan muttered. "Keep us in the air, Major!"

"We're trying, sir," he said.

"Get your chute ready," he told Nischal. The plane shuddered once more, paused and then began to descend again.

"I'm all set," she told him.

Bolan checked the altimeter again. Twenty-eight thousand feet. "We're out of time. We've got to go right now," he said, punching the button that would open the cargo bay doors.

"We're iced over completely!" the pilot yelled. "Jump clear, jump clear!"

The doors opened and immediately the wind and pelting ice slashed at them. Bolan shoved the container forward, trying to push it into the opening. Nischal leaned down to try and help, then stumbled in the gusting winds.

That was all it took for the icy air to snatch her. She

rolled toward the opening and Bolan tried to grab her but missed.

"We're going down!" the major yelled. "Get clear! We'll hold it as long as we can!"

Nischal continued the slide and Bolan saw her reach for and miss grabbing one of the support struts on the ramp. She spun around again and her chute snagged on a piece of metal sticking up from the very edge of the ramp. He couldn't hear it over the howling wind, but he could imagine the tearing sound it made.

Her eyes met his and he knew there was nothing for it. He jumped, trying to catch her, but by then she'd torn free and begun the long fall to the ground. Bolan glimpsed the ragged remains of her parachute, still hung up on the cargo bay doors and, at the edge of the ramp, their equipment. Then he, too, was free-falling into the storm.

The cold was breathtaking and his goggles were frosting over. He straightened his body, trying to pierce the darkness of the night and the storm. Long seconds passed that felt like minutes. Finally, he saw it: the telltale flicker of her shoulder light. Bolan dived straight at her, almost missed, and for a long minute, they were tumbling through the sky together.

"Hold still, damn it!" he yelled, and she wrapped her arms and legs tightly around him, locking herself in place. Bolan saw that they were at eight thousand feet, and with no clue of their location, he pulled the cord on his chute, praying like hell they didn't come down in a crevice, an avalanche zone or, worse yet, right in the middle of Nyalam, where the guards would surely have some interesting questions for them.

Nischal was trembling against him as they fell

through the storm. "We're okay," he said into her ear. "It's going to be all right."

She tipped her head back and he saw that she wasn't crying. She was laughing.

"You think this is funny?" he roared.

She didn't reply, but he could tell by the shaking of her shoulders that her mirth continued. Bolan didn't find it funny at all, but then he realized their fears about things going wrong had already come true, and he smiled wryly.

Twisting in the sky, he tried to see if he could spot the jet. In the poor conditions, it was nearly impossible to see anything. Lightning flashed all around them, a better guide to the ground than the altimeter on his wrist. He caught one last glimpse of the tail of the plane heading to the ground to the south. He shifted his grip on Nischal and reached for the flare gun tucked on the outside of his pack. He shot the red flare downward. The light was initially swallowed by the flurries of snow, then he saw it hit, flickering faintly as it bobbed in some body of water below them.

Bolan grabbed the steering toggle on his chute, bringing the canopy in on one side to pull them closer to shore.

"I hope you can swim," he yelled.

"Why?"

Nischal craned her head just as they splashed into the water. The gear from the HALO jump weighed them down, dragging them into murky depths. Bolan broke the surface, gasping for air. The water was frigid, almost cold enough to freeze over.

He'd lost his hold on Nischal when they'd hit, and he urgently searched the darkness for signs of her. The red flare floating thirty feet away was the only light. Bolan pulled a blade from his boot and cut the chute free, shoving it as far away as he could. He took a deep breath and dived under. The blackness engulfed him, but he pushed farther, deeper. He reached out for another stroke to take him deeper still and connected with what was left of Nischal's pack.

Grasping it tightly in his fist, Bolan kicked for the surface, feeling her weight still connected to the pack. When he reached the surface he pushed onto his back, pulling Nischal onto his chest. She coughed and sputtered as he swam, moving them closer to shore. After ten minutes, the bank was only ten yards out and Bolan felt like his legs were on fire. Both of them were shivering uncontrollably. Nischal began to kick, as well, and they finally made landfall. They hit the shore and the snap of the cold air hit them like a fist. Their clothing began to freeze almost immediately.

"We have to get out of these wet clothes or we'll freeze to death," Nischal sputtered through her chattering teeth.

Bolan pulled a high-intensity flashlight from his sodden pack and aimed it around the shoreline. "Look," he said, pointing. "There's a small cave or at least a place with some cover over there. Let's move."

They broke into a ragged jog, stripping their clothes the minute they were out of the wind. Bolan dug through his pack and found two T-shirts that weren't perfectly dry but were an excellent improvement over their current clothing situation. He didn't pause as he handed Nischal one of the shirts and pulled the other over his head. He also had extra pants in the bag, but they were too wet to bother with. Everything would need to be wrung out and dried once they had a fire going.

Reaching the cave, he set to the task, silently thankful that he'd managed to keep at least his personal gear together. There was enough scrub brush in the area that it took little time to get a decent base fire going. As he built it up, Nischal huddled closer to it, trying to absorb the warmth. Bolan sat next to the fire and pulled her close, rubbing her arms and legs.

"Normally, I'd object," she muttered.

"Normally, I wouldn't offer. But we're each other's best defense against hypothermia."

Her shivering began to ease and she leaned forward to rub her hands close to the flames. Bolan didn't move, watching the firelight flicker on the shadows in the cave. He studied the woman in front of him, curious about her, how they had landed together. There were few people in the world that he felt comfortable with, but her light banter had put him at ease. He noticed a small cut on her arm.

"We should dress that."

She glanced at the small wound.

"I didn't even realize I had it."

Bolan fished a small first-aid kit from his pack.

"Well, you've managed to pull out clothes and medicine from that bag… You don't happen to have a communications array, extra weapons and food socked away in there, do you?"

"No," he said. "But at first light, we'll do an inventory and see what we have left to work with."

She shook her head. "I don't have much. I think most of my personal gear is in the bottom of the lake, and the rest is wherever the plane went down."

"I bet we'll be able to find enough to get started, and by then our clothes will be dry, at least. Once we've got a handle on that, we'll go to the crash site."

"What?" she asked, incredulous.

"It's possible those pilots survived. They could be out there somewhere."

"They aren't our mission," she said.

"And our mission is going to be pointless if the Chinese find evidence of a stealth bomber in Tibet. We're going to need to do what we can to make sure they don't find any evidence."

She shook her head. "We don't have the time or the equipment to try and hide plane wreckage."

"We'll just have to improvise," he said. "Right now, we don't even know where we are for sure." He held up his phone, showing her the shattered screen. "We don't have GPS or communications to tell us our location, let alone tell anyone else. We'll have to wing it."

"That much, at least, I can help with." Nischal reached for her pants, which were drying by the fire, and pulled out a map. She carefully unfolded it to keep the damp paper from ripping. "We're isolated and we're going to need support. There's a monastery about ten miles south along the Bhote Koshi River. We can get help there and then go and look for survivors."

"No, we go after the plane. That's the mission now. We have to make it the priority or there will be war with China. No one can know we're here. After we get to the plane, we'll figure out the rest."

"You're used to getting your way, aren't you?" she asked.

"I generally do."

"So do I," she said. "But you're right. If the plane or

the pilots are found, this whole region is going to fill up with Chinese military."

"We're agreed, then?"

She nodded. "Yes. Now we'd better get some sleep. We've got a long day tomorrow."

He chuckled. "Tomorrows tend to work out that way."

5

The Russian Mi-26 helicopter had the paint style and markings of a civilian aircraft, but if trouble arrived, it was a fist inside a velvet glove. Usually used as a troop transport by the military, this one had been custom outfitted with a variety of hidden surprises, paid for by funds siphoned from other military divisions. Hidden inside the nose cone was a belt-fed .50 caliber machine gun that could be extended free of the aircraft and used to strafe ground personnel on nearly a hundred-and-eighty degree angle. On each side of the cabin, two S-5 fragmentation rockets added to the armament. The chopper's registry was civilian, too, and even the transponder code would come up as a private aircraft registered to a holding company based in the Cayman Islands that didn't actually exist. All of these, in addition to the helicopter's interior comfort, were among the reasons Nizar Vitaly used it to travel when his presence was required elsewhere in the world and why he took it to Kathmandu. Under the circumstances, it was impossible to predict what he might be dealing with, and a little local air support might come in handy.

As he stepped out of the helicopter and made his way across the pad to the waiting team, he realized he still far preferred fieldwork over the intrigue of urban intelligence. He was a hands-on kind of man, and those who knew him gave him the respect he'd earned in the field, not by playing word games at cocktail parties. The waiting men all snapped to attention as he approached, and a few of the younger ones looked nervous. It appeared that his reputation preceded him, which meant that his advance man had done his work well. Vitaly liked the unease most people felt around him—it offered an edge that few men enjoyed, let alone knew how to take advantage of. His advance man was waiting at the end of the silent receiving line.

"Fedar," Vitaly said, stopping and offering his hand. "What's the situation?"

"Vitaly, it is good you have arrived. Let's go inside and I'll tell you everything I've learned."

Fedar wanted privacy, which meant the intelligence provided by the Russian network was either wrong or woefully lacking. Which was not all that unusual in a remote location such as Kathmandu. "As you wish," Vitaly said. "Return the men to their duties for now."

Fedar snapped out an order and the men quietly dispersed. He gestured to the small offices attached to the warehouse, and they stepped inside. Although he despised the heat of Yangon, Vitaly was glad to get out of the cold wind. Kathmandu didn't have the most welcoming climate. Once inside, he found an office that seemed like it had recently been cleaned from top to bottom and emptied out. A plain metal desk and several folding chairs, along with an old coffee percolator, were about all that was left.

Fedar poured both of them a cup and sat down in one of the chairs. "It's drinkable, if barely. What they call coffee here is not all that different than highway tar."

Vitaly nodded, sipped a bit of the black brew and grimaced. He gestured vaguely around the office. "You've already cleaned this area? Is there anything missing that I need to know about?"

"No, I finished it this morning. Everything appeared to be in order, if a bit lazy. All of the files have been boxed up, locked and sent on to Moscow, but they aren't going to find anything there that helps with the situation here."

"So, what *is* the situation here?" Vitaly asked. "Was this an inside operation?"

"I don't think so," Fedar said. "I've interviewed all the personnel and accounted for the off-shift staff. I've also reviewed the security footage. Everyone was taken by surprise, and no one has gone unaccountably missing. I believe this had to have come from the outside. We found an old underground passageway that was long forgotten. That had to have been his entrance. This facility has never been breached."

"That's damn sloppy guard work, Fedar," he said. "Who else would have known about this tunnel?"

"It's not even on the retrofit plans," Fedar admitted. "No one knew of its existence. This place has been left alone for so long, procedures and drills got lax. Hell, most of the people here didn't even know what they were guarding because they weren't allowed inside. Did you know it was here?"

Vitaly laughed. "I did, and I warned Moscow about

it, but you know the situation. Everything is political now, and everyone is so busy covering their asses and keeping their secrets, it's a wonder we manage to do anything at all. How long until we can shut down completely?"

"I estimate a few weeks or so, from whenever you give me the go and a direction. The locals are stirred up, and it would be a lot easier to slip out quietly, bit by bit. It will give them less to talk about."

"You've got the go," Vitaly said. He pulled out his phone and sent a map and some additional information to Fedar. "There's the destination, too. Put someone you trust in charge of the operation and tell him he has two weeks to get it done. I don't want there to be a trace of our presence here after that time."

"And the locals on the payroll that know the truth?"

"Arrange for them to have an accident once the warehouse is cleaned out. I think a gas line explosion or something like that will suit. Be sure to pay off their families to keep them from asking questions, and if need be, pay whatever excuse they've got for a police force here to keep their noses out of it. The fewer questions, the better off we'll be."

"Easily handled. They'll all want to keep working as long as possible. Work is hard to find here, so we'll bring them in as a 'cleaning' crew once everything is secured."

Vitaly sipped more of the horrible coffee. "I'll want you with me for the rest of this mission, along with a handful of our own men—nobody local, of course. We need men we can trust. Where *do* we stand with the locals?"

"We've begun asking some questions, of course, but

I'm afraid none of us has your special touch. There are a few people left to talk to that might be of help, but I think our best bet is a man named Li Soong."

"Black market or foreign intelligence?" Vitaly asked.

"He styles himself as a professional trader, but he's a thief through and through. He moves a lot of items on the black market, mostly into China."

"Have you spoken with him already?"

"I started the conversation, but I can't give him what he wants and eliminating him would remove a valuable asset in the region. He's more than he seems and less than he thinks he is. He can be bought."

"When can I talk to him?"

"He's waiting for us now," Fedar said. "I told him to expect us."

"Take me to him," Vitaly said, setting down the half-full mug on the desk, grateful to be moving again—and not drinking the vile brew.

Fedar led him off the warehouse grounds and then through the open markets of Kathmandu to a nondescript building on the edge of the more populated areas. There was a storefront selling fabric, and Vitaly made his way around the tables stacked with cloth in what appeared to be every shade of brown and gray. The young boy behind the counter watched him with suspicious eyes and the unrepentant smile of a street urchin until Fedar stepped in front of him.

The smile faded quickly and the boy ran through a curtain and into a back room, only to return a moment later and gesture for them to follow him.

Vitaly and Fedar eased behind the counter and through the curtain. The back room itself was sparsely furnished, with only a desk and a couple of chairs. Fedar had told him on the way that the meeting place was nothing but a front. So far, he'd been unable to determine where Li Soong's true residence and place of business were located. It would be useful information, should they need to resort to more direct methods with the man. Li Soong himself awaited them in a chair in front of the desk.

He was small, almost tiny compared to Vitaly, and relaxed comfortably in his seat. Nothing about him would draw the eye in a crowd, and no doubt this near-invisibility was in part what made him an excellent thief.

"Mr. Fedar," he said, bowing from the neck. "I see you have returned, as promised."

"This is the man I spoke to you about. Mr. Vitaly."

"A pleasure, Mr. Vitaly. I am always interested in meeting new, ah…customers. How may I help you?"

Vitaly studied him carefully. "Fedar tells me that you are a man who knows things and sees things and hears things in the region."

"This is true. I know many things. The lifeblood of trade is knowledge, and one cannot make a good trade without knowing what comes in and what goes out."

"I'm looking for something that was stolen from our…storage facility on the northern side of the city. Something of great value."

Li Soong laughed softly. "Yes, I know what you seek. I don't have it." He shrugged. "Frankly, I am surprised that it was not taken from you sooner. The security at the warehouse over the past couple of years has been…less than conspicuous. Many would have paid a great deal for that information, but the trade was never brought to me."

"That's a matter for us to deal with, and no, I don't believe you have what was stolen," Vitaly said. "I don't imagine you would want the kind of attention such an item might bring, no matter how valuable it is, but Fedar seems to believe you have an idea of its location."

"So far, that has eluded me, but I can point you in the right direction, if we can agree on an appropriate price."

Vitaly looked at Fedar, who shrugged, and then back at Soong. Like a striking snake, he snared Soong by his lapels and picked him up, slamming him down onto the desk. Guards raced into the room, their weapons drawn and aimed directly at him and Fedar.

"Your guards should move back now," he said, pitching his voice very low. "I'm not a man to make an enemy of, and I respond poorly to blackmail."

"Mr. Vitaly, first you must let me go." Soong smiled. "These men are sworn to die protecting me."

"Then it looks like they'll get to keep their promise," he said, shifting his coat aside and revealing the brick of C4 that was attached on the inside. A small digital timer was counting down the seconds. "The only one that can disarm it in time is me."

"You would blow yourself up, as well," Soong said. "This is not good for your business or mine."

"You seem to think that I would mind that outcome."

There was a long, pregnant pause and then Soong began to laugh. "I like you," he said. "You play for the highest stakes of all and you are willing to bet your life for your…business." He waved his hands at his guards, who lowered their weapons and backed off.

Vitaly pulled Soong to his feet, his eyes asking the question.

"I cannot help much, but your treasure was seen on

the Friendship Highway, heading into the mountains. In exchange for a quantity of that pretty clay you are carrying, I might be able to come up with a name for you to hunt."

Vitaly glared, but Soong raised his hand. "It is not a negotiation, but there are others that I must appease to get the answers that you seek. Information comes at a price and someone must always pay it."

He reached into his coat and pulled the trigger wire out of the brick of C4 and tossed it to Soong. "There will be much more of that if you get me a name. Find me before the end of the day, or I'll assume you've failed me. I don't like being disappointed."

"I will not fail you, Mr. Vitaly," he said.

"See that you don't, Li Soong. As you said, we're playing with the highest stakes." He turned on his heels and left the store.

Once they were outside, Vitaly turned to Fedar. "Who's next?"

6

Both Bolan and Nischal were awake and waiting for first light before it even kissed the horizon with streaks of predawn gray. Their clothing was finally dry and they dressed in silence, then surveyed their pitifully small inventory. They quickly packed what little they had left and stepped out of the shelter of the cave into the cold, sharp wind of early morning. To Bolan's eye, the landscape was no more welcoming in daylight than it had been at night. He unfolded the map Nischal had managed to save and studied it once again, trying to get a bearing on about where they were, given the chaos of the jump the night before.

"At least it's stopped snowing," he said, looking up at the sky. "For now."

"Tibet is a beautiful country, but it's not a very forgiving place this time of year," Nischal said. "That snow can return quickly and with much more force. This is not a place to be without supplies."

"I'll take your word for it." He held up the map and

traced a route with his finger. "I figure if we follow the lake south, we'll come out of this bowl in that narrow valley. Hopefully, between here and there, we'll find where the plane went down."

"You know, it's not too late," she said. "It's not wildly illogical to just head for the monastery and get some help. It's not like we're loaded down with supplies, and like I said, the weather can shifts on a dime this time of year."

He shook his head. "No. We need that plane." She started to say something else, but Bolan wasn't in the mood to keep arguing, so he turned and began to follow the shoreline. His hopes that the crate containing their supplies was either floating in the lake or washed up on the jagged rocks were rapidly dashed. Nischal must have decided to take the hint because she trudged silently in his wake. They trekked south, doing their best to avoid the worst of the brutal landscape. From the map, assuming he had their position right, they were in a bowl-shaped area that bordered the north side of the mountain range between Nepal and Tibet. There were no villages marked on the map, and given what he'd seen so far, it wouldn't be surprising if no one really lived here.

Their jumpsuits made for good insulation, which was at least something of a comfort. If the weather turned nasty again, they'd have some protection. Certainly, people died in this part of the world from exposure all the time. Bolan was relatively sure that if and when they found the crash site, both pilots would be dead— assuming they hadn't ejected beforehand. Under the circumstances, he didn't think it likely.

After several hours of hiking, Bolan called a brief rest stop. They were about to leave the lake behind them, and in the far distance he could see the narrowing of the valley. "If we're going to find it," he told Nischal, "it should be along the range up ahead. That's where I last saw the little bit of light from the B-2, anyway."

"As good a place to look as any," she replied. "At the bottom of patience is Heaven."

"Are you suggesting you're out of patience?" Bolan asked. "We haven't even started yet."

"Not at all," she said. "I'm reminding myself to *be* patient. It appears that while I'm working with you, I'm going to be relying on that particular virtue a little more than normal."

Bolan got to his feet and struck southward once more, deciding to let the comment pass. He was feeling a little less than virtuous himself. With limited supplies and communication, they would be lucky to survive, let alone complete their mission. And they needed to complete their mission.

As the day began to wane, he spotted what he was looking for: blackened rocks higher up on the mountainside. He broke into a jog and heard Nischal keeping pace behind him. The B-2 had come down nose first into the nearby peaks, then had slid lower until it came to a stop about halfway up a climbable grade. The wreckage itself was spread over a fairly small area. Almost immediately, Bolan saw two things of concern: the cockpit appeared to be intact and two figures dressed head-to-toe in furs were examining the remains of the aircraft.

Bolan reached for his Desert Eagle in case the pair proved to be hostile, but Nischal grabbed his arm and shook her head.

"Give me a minute. I know the local customs."

They approached the two figures and Nischal gasped

softly, then stopped in front of them, clasped her hands together and bowed. Bolan was surprised when he realized that one was a child and the other an older Caucasian man.

"It's been a long time," Nischal said. "A very long time."

"What's this about?" the old man asked, pointing to the wreckage.

Bolan stepped forward. "Nischal, what the hell is going on here?"

"An unexpected surprise," she said. "Colonel Brandon Stone, may I introduce you to Nick Solomon?"

The name registered with Bolan after a few seconds, and his eyes narrowed. "*The* Nick Solomon? I heard you were dead."

"I am dead as far as the world is concerned." His blue eyes were sharp, and despite the lines on his face, he still seemed vigorous for a man who had to be at least in his sixties. "Which is why I don't understand why we're being properly introduced." He looked at Nischal quizzically.

"Nick, I haven't heard from you in years, though I knew you were in the region," she said. "Either way, given Colonel Stone's nature and the job we're here to do, I think it's best if everyone knows who everyone really is."

"I see," he said. "I don't suppose the two of you are responsible for this…for what's left of this B-2?"

"The storm last night was responsible for that," Bolan said. "I don't suppose you'd care to explain why you're not dead?"

"Are you going to explain what you're doing here… with a CIA field operative and a B-2 Stealth?"

"Probably not," Bolan admitted. "But then I don't have to." He eased his hand back toward the Desert Eagle. "On the other hand, I think you do. In my experience, when men like you disappear, it's often because they've changed sides. Death is a convenient excuse for no one to come looking."

Nischal put a restraining hand on his arm. "Nick's an old friend," she said. "He hasn't changed sides. He's retired."

"He's thinking that men like us don't retire, Alina," Solomon said. "Isn't that right, Colonel?"

"Something like that."

Nick Solomon was more than just an old spy. He was practically a legend in the circles the Executioner traveled in. Resourceful, smart, tough as nails and willing to go to any length to get the job done, Solomon had worked missions going back to the Cold War and in places that no longer even existed. He'd also done missions in Africa, wiping out human smuggling operations in Madagascar, and in South America, taking out cartels and drug operations like a vengeful ghost.

And he was supposed to be dead. The last anyone had heard, he'd been on a mission in Egypt that went wrong and he'd been tortured and killed. That had been more than five years ago.

"Want to tell me about Egypt?" Bolan asked quietly.

"Not particularly," Solomon said. "Any more than you probably want to talk about your missions... *Colonel.*"

"Maybe we could do the questioning part later," Nischal suggested. "When we're not out in the elements dealing with the wreckage of a stealth bomber?"

"All right," Bolan said, and Solomon nodded. "But

we will be talking more later, Solomon. There are questions that need answering."

"There always are," he said.

"Who's your friend, Nick?" Nischal asked, gesturing to the child.

"This is Raju. He helps out around the monastery.".

The boy said nothing but stared at Bolan and Nischal as though they were a definite threat. Bolan grabbed hold of Nischal and pulled her aside.

"You better start talking, and fast," he hissed. "You *knew* he was here and didn't say anything."

She shook her head. "No, I didn't. As far as the agency or the rest of the world is concerned, Nick *is* dead. He retired, but he knew the government would never leave him alone. He moved to a monastery, but I didn't know which one. In general, most of the monasteries in this region will help travelers in need, which is why I mentioned it. I didn't have a clue he was in this specific area."

"When were you going to tell me there was a super spy in the area at all? If they'd known this back in the States, they wouldn't have sent us—they could've sent him. I've seen his profile. He could have handled this all on his own."

"This *guy* is my friend," Nischal said. "He's retired, and he didn't want to be found. I can respect that, even if you can't. Sometimes people just want to be left in peace."

Bolan scanned the wreckage. "And yet, here he is."

"Yes, here I am…"

Bolan turned to see Solomon standing behind him. The man was uncannily silent. Apparently, his skills hadn't eroded much in his so-called retirement.

"My guess," Solomon said, "is that the Colonel here is worried about the Chinese spotting this wreckage when their satellites pass overhead in a couple of hours."

"That's an understatement," Bolan replied. "But I'm not telling you anything you don't already know. Let's get rid of it. Nischal, you know the area. Any suggestions?"

Nischal hesitated, then Solomon dropped his pack and pulled out several bricks of C4, tossing one to Bolan and one to Nischal.

"Let's plant these up above the wreckage and bring down the rocks to cover up most of it. Barring someone coming in on foot, it should do the trick," Solomon said.

Bolan turned the brick of explosive over in his hand and eyed the older man. There was something off about the whole situation. Bolan's instincts weren't telling him that he was in danger, but there was more to this story than Solomon and Nischal were letting on.

"Where did you get this?" Bolan asked. "Once you retire, you hardly need to keep a handy supply of plastique, and why would a monk need something like this?"

"The answer to both questions is none of your business," the former spy said. "Do you want to get to work or not?"

Bolan considered the rocky cliffs that jutted out above them. "I guess we'll get to work. The pilots are dead?"

"More dead than I am," Solomon quipped. "And nothing really salvageable, either. I suppose you lost your supply crate in the drop?"

"In the lake," Nischal told him. "We're lucky we got

out when we did. These mountains don't like giving up their secrets."

"The Himalayas are almost as tough on planes as they are on people," Solomon agreed.

They gathered as much of the wreckage as they could and placed the charges beneath the rock shelf. Each brick was set with a remote electric charge, powered by a small receiver with a battery, and a nine-volt detonator. They counted down and triggered the explosions.

The blast would be heard for miles, but they could do little about that. It seemed like there were few people in the area, anyway—other than a spy who was supposed to be dead and a boy who still hadn't uttered a single word.

"Done," Solomon said once the echoes had faded. "And well, too. Not much left to see unless you're looking for it." He wiped his hands together briskly and gestured at the boy. "Come along, Raju." They began to leave.

"That's it?" Bolan asked.

"The problem is solved, and now I will go back to my monastery. Good hunting, Colonel. Alina, it was charming to see you again."

He turned on his heel, the boy close by his side.

"Nick!" Nischal shouted. "If you can't tell us what we need, any road will do!"

Solomon paused, then shook his head. "You can come to the monastery to rest. To deny you this aid would not be in keeping with the traditions of the monastery." He glanced at the sky. "It will storm again tonight, and we have a long walk ahead of us. Let's get moving."

Sighing in relief, Nischal began walking behind Solomon and Raju, who set a brisk pace. After a minute, Bolan followed them. This mission had already become more complicated than he'd like, and adding a man like Nick Solomon to the mix could have all kinds of consequences. Was the old spy truly retired, or was he yet another player in the game?

Either way, he'd soon find out.

7

"What do you mean, it never showed up?" the President asked.

The Situation Room in the White House was silent, though the video monitors used by the Joint Chiefs were still turned on, showing a variety of tactical displays ranging from troop dispositions to satellite patterns. Hal Brognola looked over the latest reports from Delhi again, which included ground crew confirmations and complete satellite photos of the airport where the plane was supposed to have touched down.

"Just as I said, sir. The stealth bomber never reached Delhi. Our last contact with them was before they entered Nepalese air space. After that, they were flying dark."

"Damn it," the President said. "I think we may have outfoxed ourselves. That's the problem with these kinds of missions, Hal. When something goes wrong, we don't know it."

"I think it's safe to assume that they went down

somewhere in the Himalayan range, Mr. President. The satellites showed a massive storm system moving over the area in the same time period." Brognola got to his feet and pointed to the area on the satellite feed where Bolan and Nischal were supposed to have jumped. "This front and another one from the south collided over the range at about the time they were entering the area."

"And you're certain that the likely culprit is the weather and not a hostile action?"

Brognola shook his head. "I don't want to rule anything out just yet, sir, but there's no indication from the Russians or the Chinese that they knew about this mission. If they'd shot down one of our B-2s, we'd already be hearing about it. Hell, it would probably be on CNN before we heard about it ourselves."

The President raked a hand through his hair and rubbed his eyes. "Hal, what about guerilla forces in the area? Could they have the technology to pull something like this off?"

"I won't say it's impossible, but I think it's unlikely. Regionally, only the Chinese military have those kinds of weapons, and any kind of radar lock would've shown up in the B-2's systems, and they'd have either aborted or at least sent out a secure message. I believe the most likely scenario is that the pilots underestimated the severity of the weather or pushed on, anyway. Striker wouldn't have been willing to abort under the circumstances, and the plane probably crashed somewhere in the mountains."

The President considered this thoughtfully, then nodded. "In that case, it's unlikely there were any survivors—and we've got no real way to know that, either. Hal, I think we have to call this mission dead and start investigating other options."

Brognola leaned his chair back and smiled grimly.

"For crying out loud, Hal, what part of this is worth smiling about? We've lost an eight-hundred-million-dollar aircraft in hostile territory and at least four people, and there's a stolen nuclear warhead loose in the same region!"

"I'm sorry, Mr. President. I don't mean to make light of the situation. It's obviously serious, but the idea that a mere plane crash could take out Striker is, I have to admit, pretty funny. In all seriousness, though, I don't think he's dead. If the plane was obviously going down, he would've jumped early. Risky, but not necessarily as fatal as smashing into a mountain at six hundred miles an hour."

"I can't believe I'm even thinking this is salvageable," the President said. "But let's say you're right. What do you recommend?"

"I recommend that we wait. He'll find a way to contact us."

The President clicked through the feeds again and then turned back to Brognola. "I'm not willing to put all of my eggs in one basket here. I need another option."

"Yes, sir," Brognola said. "Frankly, my biggest concern at the moment is some Tibetan goat herder finding the plane and reporting it to the authorities. I don't think we want them reverse engineering our aircraft."

"Agreed," the President said. "I think we need to get in touch with Felicks Kolodoka."

The name rang a bell. "Wasn't he a Russian spy back in the day?"

"A very good one," the President said. "Now he's a

diplomat. Let's put a little pressure on the Russians and see what shakes loose. If nothing else, it may give the Chinese something to think about besides what's really happening on the ground."

"Just because we're talking to a former spy..." Brognola mused. "A good idea, sir."

"Even a President can get one of those once in a while," he said, finally allowing the ghost of a smile to cross his face.

THE SUN HAD disappeared behind the towering western mountains, leaving the sky an iron gray color that made the monastery appear almost menacing. A long, winding staircase led to a walled-off collection of pagoda-style buildings rising up the harsh face of the mountain. All the way up they passed monks, carefully hooded and silent, their eyes downcast. Bolan had expected there to be a sense of peace in this kind of place, but instead he detected sorrow and an undercurrent of anger.

They passed beneath the ruins of what had been a heavy wooden gate into a large courtyard. From the new vantage, Bolan could see that the buildings were carved directly into the mountainside, and though he was no archeologist, he'd have guessed this monastery to have been here in one form or another for hundreds of years.

Out of the blue, the boy spoke, his high-pitched voice and accent made harder to understand by the raw emotion in his tone. "You will have to forgive the fear that you see from many here," he said. "We were attacked..."

"Raju!" Solomon snapped, and the boy instantly fell as silent as the monks. "Forgive him," he said. "Our troubles are our own. Let's continue up to the main building."

Raju tucked his head down and walked ahead of the group at a faster pace. Bolan scanned the sanctuary again, and as they moved to an inner courtyard he saw the damage from the attack. Broken stones had been stacked in a pile, and the side of one building had been blackened by fire.

"What happened here?" Bolan asked.

"We were attacked. Many were killed. There is nothing else to say. The matter does not concern you. We take care of our own," Solomon said curtly.

"But why were you attacked?" Nischal asked. "This doesn't appear to be a warrior-training monastery."

"A bully doesn't need a reason to pick a fight. He just does."

"Is that why you had the C4?" Bolan asked.

Solomon gave him a cold stare, then continued to walk without answering. They entered the largest building, which offered shelter from the brutal wind. Solomon remained silent as he showed them to two rooms no bigger than jail cells. Each had a single cot, a small writing table with a basin and pitcher and an oil lamp.

"The evening meal will be served in an hour. Down the hall, you will find a place to clean up and refresh yourselves. We'll talk more later."

Solomon walked away without another word, and Nischal kept her own silence as she disappeared into her room. After a moment, Bolan entered his own small cell and set down the bag that held the meager remains of their supplies. A narrow window looked out over the courtyard below. The few monks he could see moved raggedly, as though their very steps were haunted by whatever had occurred here. All of them seemed to be in a bit of a hurry, and they kept glancing over their shoulders. These were men, he realized, who felt hunted, though why that would be the case, Bolan did not know.

Perhaps the monks' demeanor was just a result of the attack, but he had a nagging feeling that there was more to that than Solomon had revealed. He'd find out, in due time, but if the man's behavior thus far was any indication, Bolan wouldn't have an easy time getting information out of him.

Bolan stretched out on the uncomfortable cot. It was good to rest the body, even if his mind continued to work on the current situation. He needed two things right now—a phone or some other way to contact Brognola because by now he'd have figured out something had gone wrong. The other thing was more complicated.

The fact that Nischal and Solomon knew each other was *maybe* a coincidence. But that he'd just happened to be in the area, found where the plane had gone down and had some handy bricks of C4…it was too much to believe. There was more to this than either one was letting on, and as far as Bolan was concerned, secrets like that could doom a mission before it even started. He had to at least consider the possibility that there was more to the events of the past day than a thunderstorm and a plane crash.

When it was time for dinner, Bolan got to his feet and stepped into the hall. Nischal was coming out of her room at the same time, appearing a little more put-together than before and certainly cleaner. She'd obviously been grateful for the chance to rest and refresh. Even if they learned nothing else here, a dry, almost-warm place to stay for the night would help the mission all on its own.

"Feel better?" he asked as they moved down the hallway.

"A bit, yes," she said. "It's not a room at the Four Seasons but better than another night in the cave."

"Agreed."

They entered the large dining hall. Monks sat at long, low tables with floor cushions for seating. On top of the tables, large bowls of plain rice, steamed vegetables and heavy bread offered plain but filling fare. Hot tea and water were the only beverages Bolan could see. Solomon saw them enter and waved them over.

He was seated with a man in orange robes, like the other monks, but this man also sported a red sash with intricate, embroidered lettering. Bolan assumed he was the lama of the monastery. Other than a vague gesture for them to sit and eat, no one spoke. The only sounds in the hall came from eating and drinking, and even those were strangely muted. As they neared the end of the meal, the monks began to file out of the room. The lama stood, offered them a short bow and also left, while Solomon stayed put. Bolan and Nischal kept their seats, as well. They sipped on small cups of tea and waited for privacy to have a very necessary conversation.

"So," Solomon said, "who wants to go first?"

8

"I'll start," Nischal volunteered.

Bolan was surprised but kept his silence for now. Perhaps if he let her talk, she'd give something away without realizing it.

"The situation is straightforward enough, even if the circumstances aren't," she began. "A few days ago, a Russian nuke on a mobile launching platform was stolen from a warehouse in Kathmandu. It was last seen heading into Tibet."

"And your job is to hunt it down, I suspect," Solomon said. "And save the world in the process. Is that about the size of it?"

"That's the size of it," she replied. "Of course, they don't want anyone to know we're here doing it, either."

Solomon laughed dryly. "Well, you've botched that part, haven't you? What were you thinking, bringing a B-2 over the Himalayas this time of year? That was a bit reckless, wouldn't you say?"

Nischal blushed, which raised Bolan's curiosity. Why

should Solomon's scolding matter to her in the least?
"It was the best way to get us in," she said. "No one
could've predicted a storm like that, let alone that it
would be strong enough to hamper a stealth bomber."

"We played our cards," Bolan added.

"And lost," Solomon interrupted. "It happens. Now,
how do you plan to proceed? You've got no supplies,
an unfriendly country and not the first clue where to
even look."

Nischal put a hand on his arm. "Nick, a little help
would be nice. This isn't the first time an operation has
gotten off on the wrong foot. We'll make do with what
we have, but if you can assist us…"

"A phone would be an excellent start," Bolan said.
"The shelter and the meal are appreciated, but I don't
want to disturb your…retirement any more than we already have."

"We don't have a phone here," Solomon said. "Your
handlers will just have to have faith."

"Interesting," Bolan replied. "So C4 is handy, but
you don't keep a sat phone around, not even for old
times' sake?"

"That's enough," Nischal said, sending Bolan a stern
look. "Nick?"

"Are *you* asking for my help?"

"If you have help to offer, we'd appreciate it," she
said. "Yes, *I'm* asking."

Solomon turned his attention from Nischal to Bolan,
who leaned forward and placed the small knife he'd
been twirling in his fingers on the table.

"You already know we lost most of our gear, and
there's no realistic way for us to resupply. I guess I'm
asking, too, and if all I can appeal to is your sense of

professional courtesy, then that's all I've got. You were on the team once, even if you've stopped playing the game."

Solomon stared at them for a long minute. "All right, then, yes," he said finally. "I can probably help, but I don't think you'll like what I have to say."

"Why not?" Nischal asked.

Solomon took a last sip of his tea and set the cup down. "Because I think the guys you're looking for are probably the same ones who attacked the monastery."

"Why would you think that?" Bolan asked.

"The theft you're describing would require resources that very few people in this part of the world have. Jian Chen is one of them, and he has the contacts to try and sell the weapon, too, if that's his intention."

"And this Chen is the local bully who attacked the monastery?"

"He's more than a bully, Colonel. He's a regional warlord, of sorts. Lots of men, lots of weapons, some black market trade."

"And why did he attack you?" Bolan probed.

Solomon laughed. "He didn't attack *me*—he attacked the monastery. The lama refused to help him when he asked for a place to use as a base. Chen doesn't like being told no."

"I see," Bolan said. "You understand that if Chen is our man that would be an awfully big coincidence. And I—"

"Don't believe in coincidences," Solomon finished. "Of course you don't. It's part of your job to not believe in them. But I've lived long enough to understand that they happen all the time."

"Even if Chen isn't the one who stole the nuke, he

might know who did," Nischal suggested. "Many of these regional warlords are more plugged into what's going on than the intelligence community, which isn't very organized around here, even where it exists. Most intel comes through the black market."

"Look, Colonel," Solomon continued. "I understand where you're coming from, but Chen likes to flex his muscles from time to time, and the lama made him angry by defying his thugs. It's no more complicated than that. I merely suggest that he's a likely possibility for your nuclear weapon thief."

"I'm surprised that he would attack a monastery. Won't that incite the rest of the populace in this area?" Nischal asked.

"Chen is powerful but not the best strategist. He thinks his muscle will solve all situations. He doesn't realize that the monks he killed here will be the souls that haunt him to his grave."

"So how can we find him?" Bolan asked.

"I can take you to Jian's camp. Even if they aren't the ones with your weapon, they will know who is, but I believe they're your best bet."

"Okay," Bolan said.

"I have one more question for you," Nischal said with a mischievous tone in her voice.

"What's that?"

"How did you get the ambassador of Paraguay out of that harem in Saudi Arabia without getting caught?"

Solomon grinned and stood up, reaching out his hand to help Nischal to her feet. Bolan stood behind her.

"For that story, we will have to adjourn to somewhere less spiritual than the center of the monastery. Let's go back to the visitor hall and I'll tell you all about it."

They crossed the monastery, Nischal and Solomon with their heads together in conversation and Bolan following a few paces behind. As they entered the visitor hall, Bolan spotted Raju sweeping the floor. The young boy looked up as the old spy and the CIA agent walked past, and he furrowed his brow.

Bolan paused. "Don't worry, they're just old friends catching up. Nothing more."

"It's not that, sir," Raju said quietly. "It's that…he's not always the same. Sometimes he is the leader and the light of this monastery, and sometimes the soldier and sometimes…"

"And sometimes?"

"Nothing, sir. Good day."

Bolan watched as Raju retreated and Solomon and Nischal took a seat at the far end of the hall. The boy's words had only added to Bolan's sense of unease. Something was wrong and he had to figure it out before the mess they were in got any bigger.

9

Felicks Kolodoka, the old Russian diplomat, was widely known for his drinking but far more infamous for his ability to gain any information he needed—by fair means and foul. Nothing happened in the Russian empire that he didn't know about, and he was certainly familiar with all of the old, buried secrets. This was a man who could produce an army of skeletons from any closet in his homeland. Many people wanted him dead, though many were also afraid his secrets would rise from the grave. That, as much as anything else, had kept him alive far longer than most men in his position.

"Mr. Kolodoka, thank you for coming," Brognola said, shaking his hand.

The silence in the conference room was palpable as they sized each other up.

"When your White House calls, I respond. I am ever your servant."

Brognola restrained the retort on his lips and turned

to lead him into the Oval Office. They said nothing as they walked along the corridor.

"Gentlemen, please come in and have a seat," the President said.

The Secret Service agents in the room discreetly left and pulled the door closed.

"I presume you two know each other," the President said.

"We know *of* each other, sir," Brognola replied.

"If you'd like to make formal introductions, I'd be happy to have more information," the Russian said. "I think it is good to know one's...'

"Friends?" Brognola interrupted.

Kolodoka nodded. "Yes. That's as good a word as any other we might use, and better than some."

"I think that we all know as much as needed right now," the President said. "Kolodoka, we have heard some troubling things coming from Kathmandu."

"Kathmandu is not a lovely city, I am told, though I'm not sure why you're talking to me about a country that is not my own. As you know, I am merely a Russian diplomat. Do you need our help negotiating with that government?"

Brognola leaned forward and stared hard at Kolodoka. "Merely? Isn't that playing it a little fast and loose with the definition of that word?"

The Russian shrugged and offered a rather charming grin. "We are all men of the moment, and at this particular moment, I am a Russian diplomat."

"Fair enough," Brognola said. "But what you are at the moment and what you know at any other time are different things entirely. You're already aware that our concerns have nothing to do with Nepal but are about an old operation from your mother country that may have found its way into the wrong hands."

"If you could be more specific about the information, I will see what I can confirm or deny, but I cannot give you a full intelligence briefing right now. I am as in the dark as you seem to be."

The President sighed heavily. "We don't have time for these games. The clock is ticking." He turned his attention to Kolodoka. "We know there was a weapon stolen from a Russian-run facility and we have indicators that it could have nuclear capability."

"There have been some troubling reports from that area, but I can assure you that it was old, decommissioned equipment. I have it on good authority that one of our best men has already been sent to handle the situation."

"And who would that be?" Brognola asked. "Maybe we know *of* each other, too."

"Nizar Vitaly."

"Ah. I'm familiar with his work," Brognola said. "You remember, Mr. President, the incident in Serbia when the village outside of Belgrade was...removed from the map?"

"You mean when several hundred innocent civilians were slaughtered?" the President asked.

"That is not how my government would characterize that action," Kolodoka objected.

"Regardless," the President continued, "if this Vitaly was responsible, he's little more than an animal on a government leash. Have you considered that sending in someone like him might attract the notice of the Chinese? I would assume that Russia is as interested as the United States in keeping this information under wraps."

"We are aware of the complications with China, and that is why Vitaly was chosen to…address the situation. He knows that this needs to be handled quickly and quietly. Perhaps it would be best if I reached out to my government for more information and then we can meet again."

"Perhaps that would be best," Brognola agreed. "So far, the information you have seems woefully lacking in detail on what, exactly, was stolen from your facility. Are you losing your touch, Felicks?"

The Russian's eyes narrowed sharply beneath his bushy brows, then he grinned. "I have decided that I like you, Mr. Brognola. You might even be as good at your job as I am at mine."

"Anything is possible."

"When I speak to my government, what should I tell them about your response to this situation? Surely you have already sent your own…advisors to the area?"

"This is a Russian problem, Felicks," Brognola said quickly. "There are problems enough in that area. We just want it handled."

"Of course," he replied. "I'll be in touch again very soon."

Brognola and the President rose, shook hands with Kolodoka and watched him leave the Oval Office.

"What do you think he knows?" the President asked, once they were alone.

"Everything. Every last detail, down to the serial numbers on the warhead. Felicks is no fool, and he won't give up information unless he has to. And there is only one reason to send in a man like Vitaly."

The President nodded grimly. "To silence everyone who knows about the weapon."

Li Soong was as good as his word and saved his own life when he came through with the information Vitaly needed. He'd sent them north, across the border into Tibet, to meet a man named Xiu Feng—a local warlord who dealt in black market transactions and was a thorn in the side of the Chinese in the region. The drive wasn't particularly long in terms of distance, but the highway was poorly maintained and the clock on Vitaly's hunt to find the stolen weapon was ticking rapidly.

By the time Vitaly and Fedar arrived at the appointed meeting place, Vitaly's patience was already stretched thin. Xiu Feng showed up nearly an hour late with five vehicles loaded down with men. The vehicles fanned out and the warlord's guards got out, making no attempt to hide the firepower they were carrying.

Vitaly motioned for Fedar to move forward. Fedar bowed before speaking quickly in broken Mandarin. Feng seemed to understand and Vitaly took that as his signal to approach.

"I think you're looking for something of value, but I don't have this item," Feng said.

"Li Soong didn't think you'd have it, but he believes—as do I—that you have the means to find it. You know this region, according to Li Soong, and you know all the players and people. This is your territory, so you're the man I need."

"I know many things, but what you ask…"

"Maybe you're not as powerful as I was led to believe," Vitaly said. "Fedar, let's load back up and get going. We can take our money and time elsewhere."

"How much?" Feng asked.

"I don't discuss price with someone who does not believe he can perform the service I require."

"I can do this, but it may take time." Feng gestured at the wide-open sky and the massive mountains. "This is a big place to search."

Vitaly shrugged, turned and began to walk away. Fedar paused, stood wringing his hands and then followed behind. A small burst of gunfire ran along the edge of Vitaly's foot. He kept walking, turning only when he reached his truck. Another string of bullets littered the ground. Vitaly pulled his pistol as he spun and drilled a bullet into the center of the triggerman's forehead. He dropped another of Feng's men when he was foolish enough to respond. Feng lifted his hands in surrender.

"No, no…a misunderstanding," the warlord said.

"Do you have information for me or not?"

"I can help. We know these mountains better than anyone."

"You'll be well rewarded *when* we have results. Not before, and not for empty promises."

"Of course."''

"So, where could they have taken it?" Vitaly asked.

"There are sanctuaries in the mountains for travelers. We'll start with some of the monasteries and see what the monks know."

Vitaly lowered his pistol. "Good. We'll split into three groups. You send one of your men with me."

Vitaly walked back to his truck and Fedar climbed in on the other side.

"Feng is reckless, but he is easy to manage. Once he has his money he will continue to be a powerful ally," Fedar offered.

"Once we have the weapon, Feng will be of no use to us and will get the bullet in the head he should have received moments ago," Vitaly shot back. "Our orders are to leave no one who knows about the weapon and who cannot be absolutely trusted alive."

"That could leave a fairly large body count," Fedar said. "Tough to explain."

"I have no intention of explaining anything to anyone, and body counts seem to be my specialty. If they were concerned about a body count, they wouldn't have sent me."

THE QUIET OF the monastery became almost eerie as night fell. Bolan sat in his room, listening for anyone moving around. But the only sound was the breeze as it moved through the stone hallway. He opened the door and peered out before slipping into the corridor.

He continued through the complex, taking in the damage that had been wrought by the intruders. Outside, he scanned the rock face, noting a burnt funeral pyre farther up the hill. In a nook above that, he caught a glint of metal shining in the moonlight. Bolan climbed up to the remnants of the pyre and then scrutinized the cliff face again. Barely concealed by the overhanging cliff was a cache of weapons.

Dozens of crates were stacked along the walls of the natural cave. Bolan popped the top off of the first one within reach, uncovering a mound of hand grenades, packed and ready to go.

He resealed the crate and ran a hand through his hair. Why hadn't they used the weapons during the attack? Why hadn't they defended the monastery? Bolan turned to find Nick Solomon standing at the entrance of the cave.

"I knew bringing you here was a mistake," Solomon said. "You spy even in your sleep."

"What the hell is going on?" Bolan asked. "You've got enough weapons here to field an army!"

"None of this concerns you."

"Anytime I find a cave full of weapons I get concerned. If you think I could see something like this and not ask questions, you're not only retired, but you've also gone around the bend."

"Ask all the questions you like, but as I've said, it's not your concern. Your concern is if you want my help or not. If you keep asking questions, then I can show you to the door right now and you can figure it out on your own."

"You know this isn't happening without your help, and besides, I don't believe you'd do that to Alina. We need your knowledge of the region and, frankly, we need some of these supplies."

Solomon turned and headed back down the mountain, his back stiff with anger. Bolan followed, and it wasn't long before they ran into Nischal. Bolan told her the situation and watched as her jaw dropped. He was thankful someone else was as thrown as he was by the cache and Solomon's lack of interest in telling them the truth.

"Nick, you can't have all these weapons up here!" she said. "You'll invite trouble—if not from one of the warlords, then from Chinese officials. Why do you even have them? Do they belong to you, or someone else?"

Solomon shrugged. "Alina, I already told your friend, those weapons are not your problem. We have a shared problem, though—Jian Chen. Focus on that.

I'll help you resupply but on a limited inventory. I can't replace everything you've lost."

"You have enough in that cave to wipe out everyone in this region. I don't know why you're holding out," Bolan barked.

"You can either do this my way, or you are both free to leave," he said. "I'm sorry, Alina."

Solomon continued his trek back down to the monastery. "What do you think is going on here?" Nischal asked Bolan.

"I don't know. If we had more time, I'd find out, but every minute we stand here trying to figure Solomon out, that nuke is getting farther and farther away"

"So what do we do?"

"We take what help he gives us and we wait," Bolan said. "Let's get the nuke secured and then we can deal with whatever your friend has gotten himself into. One thing is for sure, whatever sanctuary and peace Solomon was looking for is long gone—if it ever existed for him at all."

10

"I believe in being thorough," Vitaly said, taking another careful slice and watching with cold eyes as the monk's blood mingled with sweat and trickled down his bare stomach. The man was tied to a crossbeam and had been raised by his wrists, the parched dirt beneath him wet with both fluids. Vitaly pulled the blade away, then traced the tip slowly up the man's chest, past the other cuts he'd already created. He paused as it reached the small hollow below the man's Adam's apple. The monk tried to tip his head away, but his exhaustion and fear from being used as Vitaly's personal piñata was too much.

He wasn't yet broken, but it would come soon. He was too young to have either the experience or the internal fortitude to fight for much longer. His quiet, contemplative life had in no way prepared him for such deeply personal and violent violations of his body.

"I'm going to ask you once more," Vitaly said. "Once more and then I'll begin working on some of your other, more fragile parts." He pulled the knife away. "Look down at your chest. See how the blood flows only a little and then stops? There is an art to my cutting that I do not think you fully appreciate yet, but you will. You see, my friend, the trick is to cut deep enough to penetrate the first layers of skin to send the right message to you and your body—but not so deep as to hit a major blood vessel or organ." He made a soft *tsk-tsk* sound and shook his head. "No, if I were to do that, you might well go into shock or die and that would not get my questions answered."

The monk's eyes followed the tip of the blade as Vitaly spoke. Fear, the Russian had found, was every bit as powerful a motivator as pain. Perhaps even more effective. People are afraid of being afraid, he thought, and there is no end to fear. Pain can potentially end, even in death. There is a powerful difference.

"Now," he said, easing the knife back down and letting the edge rest on the monk's cheek. "You know that I am willing to hurt you but not let you die, yes? So, I will ask you one more time before we move on to a more unpleasant area of your body. *Where* is my weapon?"

The monk trembled with nerves and exhaustion but remained silent. Vitaly sighed and gestured for Fedar to strip the man completely. It was an unpleasant reality that some men needed more fear than others to reach their limit. He procured another, thinner blade as Fedar removed the last of the man's clothing, revealing his most sensitive areas.

Vitaly shook his head sadly.

"A man can live for a long time without testicles," he told the monk. "Especially if the wounds are cauterized immediately. Bring the torch, Fedar."

The monk's eyes widened and the last of his resistance fled. "The weapon isn't here! We don't have it!"

"We already know that," Vitaly said. "If I'd thought it was here, I wouldn't have had to waste so much of my precious time talking to you."

"Yes, yes," he blubbered. "But there is a temple that has been rumored to be collecting weapons for months! Some are saying it is for a holy war, but that is not our way. If anyone has your weapon, it would be them."

The young monk began to weep silently, but as Vitaly slashed through the rope holding his arms, he fell to his knees and began to sob in earnest, kissing the ground and mumbling prayers of thanks.

Vitaly knelt next to him, bringing his lips close to his ear. "I need the location of this other temple," he said, making a quick gesture at Fedar, who produced a map and laid it out before them. "Where is it?"

The monk pointed out the monastery. "It's there," he said. "High up on the cliff."

The Russian wrapped a gentle arm around the man's shoulders as Fedar retrieved the map. "You've done well, my friend, and your prayers have been heard, yes?"

"Yes, yes. I prayed for mercy," the monk said. "For a release from pain. And it was granted to me."

"Not yet," Vitaly said, bringing the blade around in a swift, unseen arc. The razor edge slashed through the monk's throat, severing the artery and spraying blood everywhere. It took only a few heartbeats for the man to die. Vitaly got back to his feet and smiled. "Now you have been given a release from pain. You will feel nothing from this day forward."

He walked to stand next to Fedar and studied the map.

"What do you want done with the rest of them, sir?" Fedar asked as he gestured to the other monks who'd been tied up, gagged and forced to watch as one of their own was tortured and killed.

"Take them back into their monastery," Vitaly said, "and burn it to the ground. Remember, we can leave no one alive who knows even the slightest thing about what we're doing out here."

For a moment, it appeared as though Fedar might argue, but then he nodded crisply, turned and started shouting orders.

As the morning sun crested the top of the mountains, Bolan waited for Solomon to finish backing the old M35 cargo truck up to the rear of the monastery. The old spy had retrieved the vehicle from its hiding place in a nearby valley before dawn while Bolan and Nischal put together a small selection of ordnance and gear from Solomon's cache.

Solomon climbed out of the truck and nudged the cases they'd assembled with the toe of his boot. "Ready to go?"

Bolan stood in front of him and waited for the older man to look at him. Solomon's reputation was notorious—he'd been pivotal in the fall of the iron curtain and the end of the Cold War. Yet he'd vanished and supposedly was dead, and now Bolan had found him hiding out in a monastery packed with weapons and absolutely unwilling to answer questions. He was sure the man was linked to their current mission, but he didn't have enough information to figure out how or why.

Nick's blue eyes finally met his.

"Listen, I know all you've done," Bolan said carefully. "If you tell me what's going on, then maybe I can help. I'd *like* to help you, Solomon, if you'd just explain to me what you're doing up here. With these weapons. We're on your side."

"What's your name?" Solomon asked.

"Alina introduced us, remember? I'm Colonel Brandon Stone."

"Of course I remember. I just want to know if that's the name you're going to stick with."

"That name will do for our purposes."

The old man laughed sharply. "You're no different than I was, Stone. You're only what you want me to see at this moment. In the end, you'll do what you've been ordered to do and you'll carry out your mission, no matter who or what gets in the way. There's no trust in that, *Colonel*, just games I've been playing since you were a boy. I know all the tricks and all the lies you tell yourself to keep you going each day. The battles here are mine, not some government's. *Mine.* And I'm fighting for the people who cared when the rest of the world melted away." He stared at Bolan in silence for another moment. "Load up your gear and let's get moving."

Nischal shrugged into a field jacket and checked her pockets to make sure they were closed tight. "Did you get any more information out of him?" she asked quietly once Solomon was back in the cab.

"No," Bolan said, "and I don't suspect we will, either. He's a stubborn old goat."

"I can't disagree with you there, but honestly, I'm *worried* about him. He wasn't acting right last night. There were times when I don't think he was all there. I don't know—it was really strange."

"I'm more worried about what he has planned,"

Bolan said. "But for now, we'll go along to get along. See how this thing unfolds. We're armed again, and that's something."

He knelt down by the open crates and pulled out two Chinese QBZ-95 assault rifles and handed one to Nischal. The cases also contained four clips for each rifle and two QSZ-92 model Chinese handguns—not his favorite, by any means, but functional enough to get the job done. He offered one to Nischal, along with a handful of clips, and outfitted himself with the same for use as a backup weapon. Fortunately enough, he still had his Desert Eagle, but most of his ammunition had been lost in the jump. He only carried two magazines of the .44 caliber, and Solomon hadn't had any more in his stash. The rest of the gear was an assortment of surveillance, survival and communication equipment. Properly outfitted, both of them climbed into the truck, and Solomon stopped long enough at the gate to dissuade Raju from trying to come along or follow them. "This isn't a milk run, my boy. Stay here and look after things. We'll be back before you know it."

At least on the idea of not bringing the boy, Bolan agreed with the old spy. Whatever happened next, it would likely involve a lot of shooting.

The drive through the mountains was slow and daunting, and they were forced to stop several times to make room for cars and livestock. The road finally reached the valley floor, and the traveling was easier for a time. After the better part of an hour in the valley, Solomon stopped the truck. Ahead, a thick, heavy rise of hills was waiting for them.

"Why are we stopping?" Nischal asked as Solomon jumped out and began cursing.

"The warlord's camp is on the other side," Raju said from the back of the truck.

"Damn it, boy, I told you to stay at the monastery!" Nick cursed again. "I won't be responsible for your getting yourself killed on my account."

Ignoring the obvious for a moment, Bolan also climbed out and stepped up to the side of the truck. "How do you know?" he asked Raju.

"It's where they come this time of year," the boy said. "When full winter comes on, they will be as stuck as everyone else, but for now they can rob and steal as much as they like." He gazed at their surroundings. "It's a good place to work from."

Solomon was still muttering and swearing under his breath, and Bolan gestured for Raju to come down from the truck, which the boy did.

"How can I help?" Raju asked. "I want to."

"You could start by listening to your elders," Bolan said. "This is no place for a child."

"Well, he's here now, so I say he earns his keep," Solomon interrupted. He handed Raju a pistol and a set of binoculars, along with a small, handheld radio.

"What do you think you're doing?" Bolan asked.

"Helping," Solomon said. "He wants to help, you want help. Seems like a match made in heaven to me. All this help standing around, we may as well put it to use."

"Yes, helping," Raju agreed.

Bolan sighed. "Neither one of you is helping right now. Nischal and I will scout the area, then we'll make a plan. Right now, I want you both to sit here and sit tight."

"I'm not so old that I can't help with a simple operation," Solomon snapped. "I'll carry my own weight, thank you very much."

"No one called you old, Solomon, but I can't have anyone getting in my way," Bolan said. "If you're up to it, I'd rather you take that sniper rifle you brought along and find a good position to play God."

Solomon shook his head. "I'm not sitting this one out. I've got as much business here as the two of you, maybe more. This isn't *your* operation, Colonel Stone. We're all in this, or you can stay here with the truck."

The old spy spun on his heels, grabbing up his weapons, then stumbled slightly before righting himself and stalking off in the direction of the pass.

Bolan started out after him, but Nischal caught up and grabbed him by the shoulder. "He's a proud man. He won't stay on the sidelines any more than you would."

"He's been on the sidelines," Bolan retorted. "That's what worries me. This isn't the kind of work you can just jump back into. It takes constant training and field work to do well—you know that. Our skills have expiration dates when they're not in use. I just hope his haven't soured."

"It's his life," she said softly. "Let him be."

"Don't worry, sir," Raju cut in. "I'll stay close to him."

"Raju, he could get you killed," Bolan said.

The boy grinned up at him. "Life is harsh here, sir. If I lose my life for another, for a good cause, then it will be interesting to see what the next turn of the wheel brings me back as. I will be elevated in the next life."

Bolan shook his head. "I disagree, Raju, but I suppose you're stuck with us now. No matter what, we want to keep you safe. You can come with us, but you keep tucked out of the way."

They started in the direction Solomon had taken. Raju jogged ahead to catch up with the old man, and Nischal paced beside Bolan. Several miles later, they reached a small crest. Bolan knelt and took out his binoculars. A camp spread out below them—the base of Jian Chen, regional warlord and, hopefully, the man who'd stolen the nuke.

11

The camp reminded Bolan more of a temporary town than a rest stop for a nomadic band of soldiers. He scanned the area carefully, noting a parked convoy of large vehicles on one side of the camp, several of the trucks sporting camouflage tarp coverings.

It was still early in the day, and although there were guards on duty, the camp was fairly quiet. Most of the people who were up and about were gathered around large fires, drinking tea and eating breakfast. Bolan quickly formed a plan of attack in his mind, wanting to minimize casualties. This was very much a get in, get what they came for and get out situation. Chen had too many men for a pitched battle, and there appeared to be too many noncombatants, including Raju, who could end up injured or dead in a full-scale firefight.

Bolan outlined his thoughts to the others, then sent them to their positions. They crept down the hillside, moving from boulder to boulder, using what scrub brush there was for cover. Bolan breathed a sigh of relief as they reached their appointed spots, but it quickly changed into an exasperated snarl. Solomon didn't stop at his mark but continued moving closer to the camp. The old man paused and looked back up at Bolan, offering him a jaunty salute before disappearing over a rocky crag. The old man was going off-mission already and they hadn't even fired a shot.

After viewing the camp, Bolan had chosen to keep the one sniper rifle they had, a JS 7.62mm Chinese model, to himself. He brought the scope of the rifle up and scanned the ridgeline Solomon would be following down into the camp. He zeroed in on the first sentry, who appeared to be asleep at his post. Then he realized that the man wasn't sleeping. He'd been propped up with his own weapon. A small trickle of blood leaked from beneath the man's fur hat. Solomon had already passed that way.

Bolan knew the old spy's presence couldn't go undetected for much longer. He adjusted the scope to his first target, preparing to fire on the prearranged signal, when he heard the report of Solomon's pistol. What was he thinking? Bolan gritted his teeth, half rising to risk another look at the camp.

Every one of Chen's guards was now scanning the hillsides...and spotting him. Bolan quick-scoped the first sentry and the round took him center mass, even as the guards opened up. The Executioner hit the ground rolling. More shots rang out, ricocheting off the rocks behind him. Nischal was at his left flank, and he gave up entirely on the original plan. "Move!" he yelled, dropping the sniper rifle and bringing up his Desert Eagle as they worked down toward the trucks.

Bolan spotted the man in the closest cab seconds before he opened fire at Nischal, whose sudden appearance had startled the man into shooting. She leaped sideways as bullets shattered the large stones she was using for cover, sending slivers of rock spraying in all directions.

Bolan knew he had only a microsecond before she'd be dead. He fired the Desert Eagle twice from his prone position. The first round shattered the gun in the man's hand, and the second took him in the chest. He slumped back into his seat.

Bolan signaled to Nischal that it was time to head toward the other side of the camp. The camp was circular, so if they kept advancing, it would be hard for Chen's men to pin them down without putting their own people in the cross fire. Nischal laid down cover fire as he made his way to the truck and hauled the dead man out, using the open door as cover while he used the assault rifle to rain bullets on anyone who was targeting Nischal as she began to move forward.

A hail of bullets from a tightly clustered group of tents shattered the glass above him and he dived underneath the truck and positioned himself near the back tire. The rifle was really no use at this range, so he drew his Desert Eagle and waited for a shot. It came a moment later when a booted foot appeared beside the truck. Bolan fired, and the toe of the man's boot exploded. As he screamed and hopped into view, Bolan fired a second shot, killing him instantly.

Solomon appeared suddenly, taking advantage of the moment to shoot another assailant in the belly. He dropped his weapon and fell to the ground clutching his bleeding abdomen and howling in agony.

"Where's Chen?" Bolan yelled at Solomon.

"Heading for the nuke," Solomon yelled back. "It's here!" He gestured to the largest of the tarp-covered vehicles.

Bolan rolled out from underneath the truck and came up laying down cover fire and scanning for Nischal. She'd taken up her new position, popping off hostiles as they came into her line of sight.

Bolan maneuvered himself around the truck, then popped a fresh magazine into his rifle, tossing aside the empty one. He heard two quick shots and realized Solomon had taken out two men trying to sneak up on him from behind. Stubborn or not, old as dirt or not, apparently the man could still handle himself in a fight.

Bolan nodded his thanks for the save. Solomon gave a quick nod back and they stormed into the fray.

"We need to get to that nuke," Bolan said.

"I've got just the thing."

He dropped the rifle and pulled out a crossbow. Bolan quirked an eyebrow.

"Ever heard of nitroglycerin?"

"The stuff they used to use in dynamite."

"That's it," Solomon said, locking the crossbow in place.

"Are you saying that arrow is filled with nitro?" Bolan asked.

"No, just the tip."

He let the bolt fly and Bolan pulled him down just as it hit the rocks. The explosion rocked the valley, sending debris flying. He glanced at Solomon, who shrugged.

"Of course the rest of the bolt was lined with C4, so that added a little kick."

"A little!"

Bolan stood and saw that Chen and his men were

hightailing it in the opposite direction, leaving the truck for the taking. Nischal was moving toward them, her eyes wide with surprise at the explosion, and Raju was bouncing down the hill from his hidden perch.

"What the hell was that?" Nischal asked.

"Some cocktail Robin Hood here cooked up." Bolan reached for the quiver of bolts and placed it on the ground.

"Do you want to go after Chen?" she asked.

"No. We can deal with him later. What matters now is the weapon. If we spend all of our time chasing warlords through the Himalayas, we'll never get out of here."

Bolan inspected the truck as he counted their blessings that Solomon's improvised explosive hadn't damaged the mobile launching platform.

"It looks intact," he said. "Let's move out."

"Those idiots would never harm my little toy here," Solomon said.

A cold chill ran down Bolan's spine. There were times to scramble your words, but right now wasn't one of them. He turned to look at Nick.

"What do you mean, *your* toy?"

They stared at each other for a moment, then Solomon's expression turned from anger to resolve. Bolan heard the click of a revolver behind him as Nischal cried out and Solomon raised his pistol.

The shot reverberated in Bolan's ears. Turning, he saw one of Chen's soldiers flying backward, his handgun clattering to the earth. Solomon walked forward and put two more bullets into the fallen man. Bolan reached out and touched his arm. Solomon spun and pointed the gun at Bolan.

"You have no idea what they've done. How many they've killed and how many they're going to kill. The KGB's plans are more vast than you can possibly imagine. The damn Russians want to blow half the planet apart."

Bolan and Nischal glanced at each other. "Nick," Nischal said. "We're on your side."

Solomon's eyes darted between them. He lowered the pistol and then looked back at the dead soldier.

"We're fighting Jian Chen, Nick, remember?" Nischal asked softly. "These aren't Russians or KGB agents."

"Of course I remember! I know who I'm fighting. I just killed one, damn it! I know who I killed. I remember them all."

Solomon shook his head and walked to a large boulder, then sat down in the lotus position. He glanced at the weapon still in his hand, set it aside and began a meditation.

"Something's wrong," Nischal said.

"You think?" Bolan said. "Short of Chen returning with an army at his back, I'd say this is about as bad as things could get." He scanned the camp, but for now, everyone seemed to be keeping their heads down or regrouping. Either way, they didn't have much time to get moving.

Raju stood beside Bolan, watching and listening. The older man continued to meditate, while the bodies littering the ground steamed in the cold air. The boy began to cry quietly.

"How long has he been this way?" Bolan asked.

"Awhile now. Most times are fine, but sometimes he

won't answer to his name. Says he isn't Nick, asks how I know that name. Can you help him, sir?"

"I can try," Bolan said. "But first I have to know one thing. Did Nick take the weapon? Is he the one who stole it?"

"Yes," Raju admitted. "He said it was to protect us."

"Well, that explains how he knew it was in Kathmandu in the first place," Nischal said. "If anyone would know where the Russians were caching weapons like this one, it would be Nick. He worked a long time behind the iron curtain. Few agents had as many contacts or as much knowledge of the workings of the Russian government."

"Yes, I've seen the files," Bolan said. "I know how important he was, but I need to find out how dangerous he is *now*."

Bolan opened the door of the truck and found a satellite phone sitting inside. He flipped it open and saw both a signal and battery life. Well, that was one bit of luck.

He pocketed the phone then moved back to inspect the weapon itself. It was everything they feared and worse because, although the missile itself was decades old, the guidance system had been upgraded.

"The hardware on this…it's newer than the original design," Bolan said, gesturing for Nischal to come take a look. "This isn't just a weapon that was hidden and forgotten. This was made for use today."

"But why? They've already got enough nukes to blow up the world twice. Why make old missiles better when they have a whole arsenal of new ones?"

"Probably to sell to some of our Middle Eastern friends, who would be perfectly happy with old nukes with updated guidance systems. There are a lot of heavy-duty weapons missing from the USSR. Mostly ground-combat stuff, but even missiles, tanks and helicopters disappeared in the chaos. There are those inside Russia who will sell them to the highest bidder."

"What do you think you're doing with my weapon?" Solomon asked from behind them.

"We're going to take it to safety," Nischal said. "You know that's why we're here."

"I need it. It's the only way to keep the Chinese at bay. Tibet has suffered enough. Haven't you seen that? These people won't need to fight anymore. They need some peace." He patted the side of the platform. "This will ensure that Tibet will finally be free."

"Nick," Nischal implored him. "There will never be peace in Tibet if there is a nuclear weapon on its soil. The Chinese will never stand for it. They'll attack."

"Then they'll die," he said. "And they know it."

"Yes, some will die," she admitted. "But if you launch this, you won't be stopping the war—you'll be starting it. You'll give every trigger-happy country in the world an excuse to launch, and you'll still be facing a billion angry Chinese soldiers storming into this country."

"They'll keep coming, and then even more in Tibet will die," Bolan added. "Tibet will have lost its chance for freedom."

"No!" the old man snarled. "With the Chinese here, Tibet will never get a chance to be free."

"Solomon, you're a soldier. You know how this works," Bolan said. "The decisions get made by men a long way from the front lines. You're talking about starting the next world war. Instead of saving lives, you'll be throwing them away. You cannot win Tibet's freedom this way. China has too strong a hold."

Solomon's shoulders slumped in defeat. "Perhaps you're right. We'll take it to the monastery and resupply, then I'll help you move it to your extraction point. It's the least I can do after deceiving you."

"Our extraction point is a long way off already," Bolan said. "Delhi, India, to be exact. We can't go direct from here?"

"Not unless you want to carry it on your back," Solomon snorted. "We'll need full fuel tanks and more supplies just to make it to Kathmandu."

Bolan considered this, then nodded. "All right, let's get out of here. The sooner we leave, the better off we'll be."

Nischal glanced around at the corpses and the wreckage in the camp. "Let's hope so."

12

Fedar ordered the nearest men to drag the dead monk's body out to the courtyard as Vitaly holstered his side-arm.

"So, the weapon was here, then, yes?" Vitaly asked.

"It was here," Fedar confirmed. "We got positive trace readings on the Geiger counter." He stretched his tired back. "Plus, whoever is running the show up here—and it's not one of these monks, I'll swear to it—has stored enough weapons in that cavern up there to start quite a war. Nothing too heavy, but he's obviously planning something pretty big. Do you believe he's coming back?"

Vitaly glanced up at the cliffside. "He's coming back. No one would leave a weapons' cache like that unattended for long."

"I agree," Fedar said. "He didn't think he was leaving forever. So, do we keep questioning the monks and try to find him? How do you want to proceed?"

Vitaly smiled. "I think we can afford a little patience

now. Move the rest of the monks into the dining hall and keep them under guard. Let's get our men ready, so we can give our mysterious friend a proper homecoming."

Fedar grinned in reply. "I'm sure that can be arranged. And then we can be done with this mess and on our way home."

"Indeed. On our way home with plenty of extra money in our retirement accounts. Have the men empty the cavern and load the other weapons into the trucks. I'm sure Li Soong will have a way to market those for us in return for a fair share of the proceeds."

"I was thinking twenty-five," Fedar said.

Vitaly shook his head. "I was thinking zero, but we've got a little time. Perhaps you can convince me to let him live."

"I can only try."

Xiu feng stood on the rim of the crater and watched as his men created havoc below. This village was the last place to procure supplies before they trekked into the true high country, where the weather and the land often conspired to kill the prepared and unprepared alike. The natural crater created a fortress-like wall for the settlement, which consisted of a small Buddhist shrine, a monastery and a handful of buildings set into terraced steppes in the rock face. The men were mostly charging through houses and knocking things over. He'd told them to keep the actual violence to a minimum and bring him anyone who might have information.

Two of his soldiers moved toward the monks who sat in silent meditation in front of the shrine.

"No," Feng said, holding out his hand to stop his

men. "Leave them and the monastery alone. Spread the word."

"Vitaly said to question everyone," one of the soldiers reminded him. "He does not seem like the kind of man who is used to being disobeyed."

"Vitaly," Feng said quietly, "does not have to live in these hills after this is over. Only a fool forgets that. The people will answer our questions because we have shown restraint, and Vitaly will take whatever answers we find. He cannot do this without us."

"Sir, look." The man pointed to the jagged road at the base of the mountains.

Feng didn't need binoculars to recognize the gift that was heading his direction. "You see, when you are patient, good things come to you," he said. "Move the men into position. Let's go and get our reward."

Feng paused long enough to turn to the shrine and offer a silent prayer and a nod of acknowledgment to the monks, who maintained their silent, meditative poses. Still, he knew they'd heard what he'd said, and the word would spread that he had withheld when he could have used force.

Such an action would ensure better cooperation in the future with the tough locals in the region. Feng turned back around and headed down the steppes toward the road. A gift should be received properly, and this was one he didn't dare miss out on.

Li Soong traced his fingers across the Ming vase. The moon flask was so beautiful and rare that Soong wouldn't display it. He kept it in his vault with the rest of his true treasures. He liked what Kathmandu had done for him and, more important, what it had done for his collection. He carefully replaced the flask on the shelf. The last one auctioned on the open market had sold for more than a million dollars and it was a great deal smaller and less intricate than this one. Someday, perhaps, his son would sell it, but Soong would not; the acquisition of the piece was his prize, and its financial value was only a way of keeping score.

He stepped out of his vault, locked the heavy door carefully behind him and saw one of his spies was waiting silently, his head bowed.

"What have you heard?" Soong asked.

The man raised his head. "Exactly what you suspected, sir. These men—Vitaly and Fedar—are not on any of the Kremlin's protected lists and not appointed or elected officials of any kind. According to our sources, Vitaly leaves no witnesses to report his activities or results. So that gives you an idea of what kinds of missions he gets sent on."

"But you're certain he works for the Russian government?"

"Yes, he works for the Russian Foreign Intelligence Service. He's ex-military, too."

Soong paced through his store, running his fingers along the merchandise as he walked. He was a wealthy man already, but men like Vitaly threatened his business and, more important, his collection. Worse, a man like Vitaly would consider Soong a definite loose end and would no doubt be back to tie it up before he left the area.

He turned back to his spy. "I think we must take some precautions."

"What do you want me to do, sir?"

"This warehouse of theirs...we've been watching it

for a long time, but I think there are too many people working there. We should help Vitaly with this situation. Move our people into the warehouse and get the others out, except any Russians they've left behind. Do it quietly."

"I don't understand, sir. How will this help us with Vitaly?"

"Vitaly will understand," Soong said. "After all, he would hate for the contents of that warehouse to fall into the wrong hands or, worse still, land on the evening news in Beijing. I suspect having our people in play will go some way toward ensuring his cooperation in the future."

"And if he isn't cooperative?"

"Then we'll try something else. A wise man once said that necessity is the mother of invention."

THE TRUCK ROCKED back and forth on the pitted track that passed for a road in this part of the world. Bolan drove with Solomon by the passenger window and Nischal and Raju squeezed between them.

Bolan watched Solomon out of the corner of his eye. The old man appeared to be lost in his own thoughts. Something about him intrigued Bolan. Perhaps it was the years of dedicated service to similar causes. They'd fought different wars at different times, but their missions had been essentially the same in purpose: stop the bad guys any way possible and make the world safer for everyone else.

No matter what the cause of his fascination, Bolan knew one thing for certain—Solomon was not functioning at a hundred percent. And he was still keeping secrets from them. Secrets that could make or break this mission if Bolan didn't wrest them out of the older man soon.

"You know, Nick," Bolan said carefully, "I'd like to help you if I can. If you tell me what you were really trying to accomplish, perhaps there's something I can do. Were the warlords threatening the monastery? If so, I'm certain we can create a deterrent that doesn't include a nuclear device."

"Yeah," Nischal chimed in, catching on to Bolan's strategy. "Nick, whatever it is, we can help. We can keep your name out of the report. As far as Washington is concerned, the weapon was stolen by a warlord or someone looking to make a profit. They won't care about anything else once the nuke is recovered and the stockpile revealed."

"You like your proverbs, Alina," Solomon muttered. "So let me put it this way—better than the young man's knowledge is the old man's experience. I'm old, and neither one of you would understand."

"Fair enough," she said. "But I'd remind *you* that goodness speaks in a whisper, while evil shouts. A nuke is a very loud shout, Nick. If you give us a chance, explain things, then maybe that would help us to understand."

"I think you should..." He trailed off, staring out the window at the passing mountains.

"What?" Bolan asked.

"Drive faster," he said. "Much faster!"

Solomon pointed up the hill just as bullets began to rain down on the truck.

Nischal peered out the window. "Shit. It's Xiu Feng, a local warlord. Brutal reputation. Drive!"

"Just another day in Tibet," Nick said, laughing.

Bolan downshifted, trying to force a little more torque out of the neglected old engine. The truck lurched forward as another hail of bullets shattered the driver's side window. Bolan shifted again as two jeeps caught them at the top of a rise, slamming into the side of the truck. Bolan gripped the steering wheel hard, trying to keep the truck on the tight road. He pulled out the Desert Eagle and fired off two quick shots, hitting his first target. The man flew off the side of the jeep and tumbled under the rear wheels of the truck.

The second jeep rammed them again, from behind, while more bullets were flying from the vehicle next to them.

"Take the wheel!" Bolan yelled at Nischal.

She leaned over and did as he said, and Bolan popped open the door, slamming it into the man who was in the midst of making a leap from the jeep to their truck. He flew backward, landing in his own vehicle.

"Stay down, Raju!" Solomon shouted into the cabin.

"Nischal, take over," Bolan said, then he jumped into the jeep beside them.

The man he'd hit with the door earlier popped back up, delivering a hard uppercut to Bolan's jaw. Nearly toppling over the open side of the jeep, Bolan grabbed at the edge, then used his own momentum to reverse direction and plant a sidekick into the man's chest.

He screamed once as he fell onto the hard-packed road.

The driver turned, a revolver in his hand, and fired. Bolan dodged sideways, narrowly avoiding taking a bullet. He reached out, striking like a snake, and put a bone-crunching wrist lock on the arm holding the weapon. A sharp reverse and twist, and the wrist broke easily.

The driver screeched and dropped the gun. The jeep began to swerve wildly, losing speed, as they fought for control. They were no longer keeping pace with the truck, and the second jeep passed them by.

This was no place to get pinned down in a firefight.

Bolan maneuvered around his opponent, reached down and snapped the driver's neck, then flung the door open and pushed the man's body out as he dropped into the seat he'd just occupied.

Bolan floored the gas, quickly closing the distance between himself and the second jeep. They saw him coming, but there was little to be done on the narrow road as he slammed into them. One of the gunmen swung around and began firing, forcing Bolan to swerve to keep the damage to a minimum and avoid getting hit. He sent two shots from the Desert Eagle in their direction, causing them to duck for cover. He hit the gas and rammed them a second time, then forced his jeep around and smashed into them sideways. The sounds were atrocious—metal against metal, the rough banging of a vehicle bouncing over rocks and pits in the road.

They shoved back against Bolan, trying to jam him into the hillside. Ahead, Nischal had managed to create some distance and the truck pulled around a bend in the road. Bolan slammed into the other jeep once more, and this time, there was no room to swerve. As Bolan floored his own brakes, the other jeep plummeted over the side of the cliff.

He sped up once more, feeling certain that whatever lay ahead would be just as dangerous, if not more so.

13

Vitaly peered at the mountain road through binoculars as his prey approached. Although it was unclear exactly why this mysterious man had stolen, then lost and was now returning with his nuclear weapon, what mattered was that he was within reach. In a short time, Vitaly would recover the weapon, clean up any witnesses and be on his way back to Kathmandu. So far, the hunt had been relatively straightforward and little had gone wrong.

Which was why, when he saw Feng and his men interfering, he cursed under his breath. The lack of communication between them was an unforeseen problem, but phones and radios were essentially useless out here. Nonetheless, even Feng should have realized it would be better to follow the truck and take it when it stopped than attempt to force it off the lousy road in a running gun battle. Vitaly would make certain Feng paid for his stupidity. He gestured for Fedar to come and watch.

The battle unfolded below. There was nothing ordinary about these people, Vitaly realized, as the driver of the truck jumped into one of Feng's jeeps. These were professional, combat-trained operatives of some kind. There was no way to say for certain how many were involved, but it was clear that he was going to be dealing with more than half-wit, untrained locals.

As Feng's men lost control of the situation, Vitaly shook his head and turned to Fedar. "Gather the men together. We're going to have to go down there and intercept them before this gets completely out of hand."

"Sir," Fedar replied with a sharp nod and moved off, shouting for their soldiers to fall in.

With any luck, whoever it was down there would be so focused on Feng's men that he could get into position and take the nuke, ridding himself of all the other parties in one action. If he was really lucky, Feng would kill the thieves, and then he'd only have the ugly warlord to remove for his troubles. That would ensure a positive end to a day that currently looked pretty grim.

"We're all set, sir," Fedar said.

Vitaly turned away from the vista below. "Let's get down there and into position. When that truck arrives, I want us to hit them with everything we've got. Let's end this now."

Bolan rocketed through the gears on the jeep, upshifting every chance he got, downshifting as he hit curves, tearing up the road and trying to catch the truck. Whipping around the third blind corner he had to slam on the brakes. The truck was stopped in the road, surrounded by one of the bands that roamed these mountains. Nischal and Solomon were already out of the truck, with guns pointed at their heads and their hands raised in surrender. There was no sign of Raju. Hopefully, the boy had made himself invisible inside the truck. Bolan jumped out of the jeep and walked forward, showing his open hands.

The man who appeared to be in charge—Feng, he assumed—separated himself from the group and approached him. "You must be one of the Americans we were told was tearing up this mountain. There are those who would pay plenty just for the knowledge of American military forces in this country, let alone the nuclear weapon you're hauling."

Bolan spoke cautiously. "People will pay for a lot of things, but you have to be able to collect. I want to be clear with you now. Those are my friends and that weapon on the back of that truck is coming with us. There are no other alternatives available to you."

"I don't think so," Feng said. "I think I will turn you all in, including the weapon, and collect a nice reward for my troubles." He peered back down the road. "Though I am unhappy that you have killed several of my men, and you will have to pay that debt yourself before I turn you over to the authorities."

Over the man's shoulder, Bolan saw Solomon wink at him and knew this was going to get ugly in a hurry. He had to keep the man talking and focused on him. "You're nothing more than a warlord who terrorizes this part of the mountains. If you go to the real authorities here, say the Chinese in Nyalam, they'll just kill you along with the rest of us. So who's holding your leash?"

"Leash?" the man said. "You think I am someone's dog?"

Bolan shrugged. "I think you're someone's *lap* dog."

The man's face turned an ugly red and he stepped closer to Bolan.

Over at the truck, Solomon played the old and feeble card, leaning in on his captor for support. The man moved his pistol out of the way and it was all the opening the spy needed. He yanked the gun out of his hand, reversed field and drove an elbow into the his face, then shot the man closest to Nischal in the head. He went down in a spray of blood and bone.

Solomon's captor was on the ground now, holding his gushing nose, and Solomon put a round in him for good measure.

Startled, the man in front of Bolan turned and began running toward his men while Nischal and Solomon hit the deck, rolling beneath the truck and out the other side. Bolan laid down fire with the Desert Eagle and took cover on the far side of the truck.

The warlord, rather than continue the fight, jumped up into the cab of the truck, shouting for his men to climb on. He put it in gear and started down the road. Nischal and Solomon dived into the ditch for cover as their assailants fired down on them, while Bolan used the cover of the jeep's passenger door.

Solomon left the ditch and tried to make it to the jeep, coming within feet before a bullet caught him in the leg, sending him tumbling to the ground.

"No!" Nischal yelled, breaking cover herself.

"Get back in the ditch!" Bolan ordered, reaching out from behind the door. He grabbed Solomon by one arm and dragged him behind the jeep.

The warlord's men stopped firing as they increased the distance between them, and Nischal took the opportunity to sprint over to Bolan and Solomon. She tried to assess Solomon's wound, but he kept shoving her hands away.

"We need to get in the car," the old spy said. "Now."

"You're hurt," Nischal protested. "Let me take a look."

He gripped the bumper and pulled himself to his feet. "It's barely a scratch. We can't let them get away with that weapon. And I think Raju's still in there."

"If he says it's a scratch, it's a scratch," Bolan said as he helped Solomon into the back of the vehicle. "Nischal, you drive."

She hesitated, then got behind the wheel and tore off after the nuke.

As they drove, Bolan examined Solomon's leg. The older man hadn't been downplaying his injury. The bullet had plowed a furrow in the side of his thigh, but it hadn't gone deeper than the skin. It was bleeding a bit but not too badly. Solomon had survived far worse, without a doubt.

"What were you thinking?" Bolan asked, wrapping the wound with a strip of cloth from his T-shirt. "You should have waited to move until they were out of range."

"Well, I was thinking that they were driving off with a nuclear weapon and likely to disappear into the damn mountains with it." He grunted as Bolan tied off the makeshift bandage.

"You might have thought about that before *you* stole the damn thing in the first place," Bolan replied. "Then we wouldn't be in this mess to begin with."

Nischal gunned it down the hill, trying to catch up. The warlord was doing his best to turn the road into an obstacle course as he left the main track and headed off onto one of the side roads that was littered with boulders and old, broken-down vehicles and was barely wide enough for a wagon, let alone a mobile nuclear launching platform.

Bolan glanced behind them. "Nischal, I think we may have more company."

"Who?"

"I'm not sure, but you'd better drive faster because any second now, we're going to be in range of that fifty caliber they've mounted on top of their SUV."

"Shit," she said. "Wouldn't you know it?"

"What?" he asked.

"I left all my fifty cals back in the States."

KOLODOKA SETTLED INTO the plush leather of the jet with a Kauffman Vodka rocks in one hand and a file in the other. He tipped back the glass, leaving ice as the only evidence that he'd been drinking. The vodka was expensive at more than two hundred dollars but worth every penny. The flight attendant filled it up again moments later. His instruction to the flight staff had been to never leave him with an empty glass.

He flipped open the file with Vitaly's picture laminated inside the front cover. On many of the pages inside, specific details had been redacted. Of course, Kolodoka knew the whole truth without needing to read the blacked-out information. It was his job to know. In Vitaly's case, each black line had a body—or mountain of bodies—attached to it, left to rot in some backwater village most of the world had never even heard of.

The flight attendant came back to pour again, but he waved her off and pulled out his laptop. He extracted the jump drive hidden in his ID lanyard and popped it into the USB port, bringing up the warehouse inventory. He cursed himself for not moving the materials sooner. Many of the weapons stored there were already promised to various organizations, and he'd taken deposits. His credibility would gain him a little time, but eventually his buyers would want their orders filled.

He knew he would need to get control of the situation quickly before the Americans or the Chinese discovered what was really going on. He would have to come up with a story for Moscow, too, but stories for Moscow were his specialty. This might even work to his advantage if he could keep the Americans out of it. The real problem was Vitaly.

He flipped through the file again and thought about what Vitaly would do to recover the nuke, how far he would go to retrieve it and ensure no witnesses remained. Unfortunately, he already knew Vitaly would do whatever he deemed necessary to accomplish his mission. Kolodoka consulted another electronic document, then picked up the phone and dialed a man he was certain could be bought and would be helpful. He called himself Li Soong, though the gods only knew if that was the man's real name. Kolodoka suspected not.

Soong answered on the second ring. "Mr. Kolodoka, sir. What an unexpected surprise."

Kolodoka was calling from a scrambled phone line on a private jet, so the fact that Soong knew it was him was more than a little surprising. "Li Soong," he said, keeping his tone neutral. "How did you know it was me?"

"I had a feeling I'd be hearing from you," the man replied. "And no one else has this particular number, as I only gave it to you."

"Clever man."

"Clever always pays dividends," he quipped. "As I said, I expected to hear from you. I had the opportunity to meet your friend. He's not a very pleasant person, and my sources north of the border tell me he's making himself known in all kinds of ways. The Chinese have set the guards around Nyalam on high alert and they're going to be sending out patrols very soon."

"Vitaly is not a friend of mine, and I never send pleasant people to recover my missing property. I send successful ones, who know how to behave."

"I see," Soong replied. "So Vitaly did not come at your behest, then?"

"No," Kolodoka replied. "He's working for…someone else. I may be in need of your services."

"Anything for an old friend, of course, but with something this delicate, the price tag will be high. And you can count on Vitaly ensuring that the situation is as delicate as fine crystal. What are you offering?"

"Something better than money."

"Better than money?" Soong asked. "I am intrigued. What do you have?"

"Something special for your collection," Kolodoka said. "I guarantee you'll love it or we'll discuss cash terms when I arrive."

"Hmmm…we shall see. When do you wish to meet?"

"I'm on my way now, but it will be a while. I'll call you when I land. And Soong, I know the temptation is to do something bold, to grab all of the profits you can for yourself in these unexpected circumstances, but do yourself a favor and stay out of this one. Many governments are involved in this game, and if you get caught in the middle, the blame may very well land squarely on your head."

"I'm here only to serve. Call when you arrive."

"I suspect you'll know before my wheels touch the ground, but I'll call all the same."

Kolodoka hung up the phone and waved the flight attendant over. She filled his glass again and he tipped it back, swallowing the rich vodka and enjoying the faint burn of it on the back of his throat. Finally, he handed her the glass and she walked away, her hips swaying beneath the thin, midthigh velvet of her dress.

He put his head back on the cushions and watched the clouds float by under the plane before closing his eyes. He kept them closed until Vitaly's past came creeping in to interrupt his daydreams. He waited for the pictures and the screams to fade. He'd been dealing with men like Vitaly all his life, and some would say he was the greater evil because his empire was so much larger, but Kolodoka knew better. He collected secrets like Soong collected trinkets and art, and certainly he profited by those secrets, but he was not a vicious killer. This time, he intended to stop one…one who'd been set loose by Mother Russia herself. Sometimes, protecting one's country meant killing its own agents. Vitaly was no longer part of the big picture.

Kolodoka closed his eyes again and fell asleep.

14

Brognola paced the carpet of the Oval Office and waited
while the President continued to page through his daily
paperwork. A decisive knock came on the door, and the
President called out for the person to enter. The man
they'd been waiting for, a high-level functionary who
worked directly for the Chinese ambassador came strid-
ing into the room. Ru Quan was tall and reed thin, with
short-cropped black hair and intense eyes. He radiated
irritation, though it may have been a pose.

Silence pervaded the office for a long minute as the
three men looked from one to another. Quan finally offered his hand to the President, then Brognola.

"Mr. Quan, I'm delighted you could come and join
us for another discussion," the President said.

Brognola noted that he didn't offer for Quan to sit
down, so the three men remained standing.

"Forgive me, Mr. President, but I suggest we dis-
pense with formalities and discuss the military actions
that both the United States and Russia are currently

engaging in, both in Kathmandu and Tibet, which is, as you know, part of the People's Republic of China."

The President began to shake his head, but Ru Quan held up his hand. "Before you begin the usual litany of denials, let me say that we already have evidence that military personnel, disguised as mercenaries, have been spotted in Tibet. So, might I again suggest we skip the formalities and the fake surprise? Let us instead discuss what your people are doing in the region."

Brognola waited for the President to speak. If the Chinese had any hard evidence, they wouldn't be talking to Quan. They'd be talking to the ambassador himself or, more likely still, the top officials in the Chinese government.

"Mr. Quan," the President said, "I can tell you that we've also noted some activity in that region, but sending in troops of any kind would be a violation of several treaties and would stand in the way of the friendship between our nations."

"Then you would deny any knowledge of a spy plane over Tibet," Quan stated flatly. "We have a preliminary report suggesting that a US plane was seen heading in that direction just prior to a major storm. It would be typical for an advanced military like yours to use the storm as cover to spy on another nation."

He was fishing, and both Brognola and the President knew it.

"I can assure you, Mr. Quan, that we did not send a spy plane into Tibet or Kathmandu. We have our own intelligence analysts working on some of these same reports, but most of the information is unreliable at the moment—as I'm sure yours is."

Very smooth, Brognola thought. The B-2 Spirit was

not technically a spy plane but a long-range bomber. In politics, the precision of language was crucial.

"Certainly, should we learn of anything that clarifies matters, I will contact your office and share it with you immediately," the President continued.

Quan looked as though he wanted to say more, but he only nodded sharply. "You have forty-eight hours, Mr. President, to come up with some reasonable explanations, but don't expect that we will be idle in the meantime. Should we find evidence of US personnel on the ground in Tibet, the repercussions could be… quite serious."

"Is that a threat, Mr. Quan?" Brognola asked.

"No, Mr. Brognola. It is a vow to…look into matters more deeply." Quan turned on his heel and exited the Oval Office, all but slamming the door behind him.

"What do you think, Hal?"

"I think he's pissed, but his intel is lousy at this point. Still, he's serious enough. China is touchy about Tibet. They know most of the world, including us, would prefer Tibet to be treated as a free nation."

The President returned to his desk and sat down. "I think we need to send in a strike team."

"Sir, that will only increase our chances of getting caught in the middle of this," Brognola cautioned. He took a seat across from the President. "The more boots we put on the ground, the more likely we are to attract attention."

"But at this point, we don't know if we even have anyone alive over there, Hal. All we know is we've got a missing stealth bomber and two operatives who may well be dead. Given what Quan suggested, we have to consider that the plane crashed or was shot down—

and the damn Chinese are looking for the wreckage right now."

"I understand your position, sir," Brognola said. "But I don't believe any plane crash could kill Striker. He's too tough to die like that. He'd survive it out of sheer spite, if nothing else."

The President shook his head. "Your assurances aren't enough, but I'll give them twenty-four hours. If we haven't heard from Nischal or Striker in that time frame, then we'll have to send in another team *and* come up with something to tell the Chinese."

Brognola nodded. "I'll work on a cover story, sir, but they'll turn up. I know it."

"I hope for all our sakes that you're right," the President said. "If Striker somehow manages to pull this off and not get caught by the Chinese at this point, he's more than tough—he's a damn miracle worker."

Brognola forced a grim smile. "That's his specialty."

NISCHAL SKIDDED AROUND a small boulder, throwing Bolan and Solomon into the door.

"Are you *trying* to kill us?" Bolan asked.

"Yes, that was my grand plan all along," she snapped. "Secretly have someone steal a nuclear weapon, and then, in an effort to get it back, kill you with my poor driving skills." She pointed to the road ahead. "There they are!"

"How much farther until we hit Nyalam?" Bolan asked.

"At this pace, we'll be out of the valley within an hour or so, and this secret will be on CNN," Nischal answered as she closed the distance between themselves and Feng's men. Then the shooting started again in earnest. Bullets ricocheted off the jeep's steel frame and Nischal was forced to swerve wildly, trying to keep them from getting shot to pieces. Out of some necessity, she slowed down again.

"Well, this seems familiar," Solomon said.

"No kidding," Nischal yelled.

Bolan chambered a round in his Desert Eagle. Solomon grabbed the 9 mm that was tucked in his belt. Nischal hit the gas, driving off-road to get around the convoy, leaving what was left of the muffler on a rocky outcropping that was a little too tall for the jeep.

She continued to pick up speed until they crossed a small wooden bridge where the road had been washed out.

"This will do," she said, hitting the brakes and spinning the jeep sideways, blocking the far side of the bridge.

"This is your plan?" Bolan asked.

"We have to make a stand somewhere," she said. "This is about as good as it's going to get, and either way, we could be spotted by a Chinese patrol any minute."

The argument was over before it started as the bullets started flying again. Bolan shoved open the door and started shooting. Feng and his men had stopped short of the bridge and were fanning out to surround them. The SUV with the mounted rifle was approaching in the distance. This area was going to get crowded fast and it would be impossible for the three of them alone to come out on top.

"This isn't going to work," Bolan yelled. "Run up the wash and get to cover!"

"I'm not leaving them with that truck," Nischal said.

"They aren't getting this nuke, damn it. And we have to help Raju."

"If we don't get out of here, they'll get the nuke, Raju and you both," he barked. "Get to cover *now*!"

Bolan laid down suppression fire as Solomon grabbed Nischal's arm and pulled her up the wash. Bolan continued to shoot, switching out weapons until they were far enough away to return the favor by keeping the heads of the bandits down as Bolan took up a new position behind a large boulder.

VITALY WATCHED THE firefight develop, waiting for it to come to a slow halt in front of him before he got out of his truck and gestured for Fedar and the men to follow. Very little could get in his way now. He approached Feng, who stood at the rear of the convoy with some of his men.

"What's the situation here?" Vitaly asked, startling him.

"There you are," Feng said, apparently playing the innocent. "I wondered when you'd turn up."

"I'm certain you did," he replied. "I believe my instructions, if you were to capture the weapon, were to guard it until I arrived—not take off down the road with it."

"If we hadn't been attacked, I would've followed your instructions," Feng objected. "Three operatives attacked us and I felt it was wiser to keep the weapon away from them and head to Nyalam, where we could easily meet up."

"I see," Vitaly said. "So, you and your men were rerouted by three operatives? You're obviously a force to be reckoned with, Feng." He sighed and shook his head. "Where are they now?"

"They went up the wash and have taken cover in the rocks there. As soon as we've pushed them back a little farther, we can move the jeep out of the road and then you'll be free to take the weapon wherever you like." He pointed toward the horizon. "The Friendship Highway is only an hour or so away. You could be back in Kathmandu by late tonight, if the weather holds."

Vitaly glanced at the sky, which held low clouds, but the weather wasn't of serious concern to him at the moment. No doubt the operatives were Americans, and it was likely that one of them was the man who'd stolen the weapon to begin with. They'd have to be dealt with, but Vitaly believed in taking care of one problem at a time.

"Feng," he said, pitching his voice low. "What did we agree on as a price for your services?"

He smiled. "We did not agree on a price. You only promised that I would be well rewarded." He pointed at the mobile platform. "I think you must believe I have done as much or more than anyone else could have in this same situation."

"I agree completely, Feng," Vitaly said. He snap drew his handgun and shot Feng in the forehead.

The look of surprise on Feng's face was priceless as his body tumbled over backward. Before his men could react, he shot Feng's personal guard and Fedar gestured for their men to cover the others.

"Your orders, sir?" Fedar asked.

"Kill them all."

Some of Feng's men escaped into the hills, but when most of them had been taken out, Vitaly's men pushed the jeep off the road, clearing it for their soon-to-be-leaving convoy.

Vitaly smiled in grim satisfaction. He had the weapon and the American agents were hiding in the hills. He could deal with them at his leisure, as soon as the weapon was properly secured. In fact, he anticipated that they would follow him—were under orders to do so. They would be part of his final cleanup here before he left the region.

All in all, things were going fairly well.

DAIYU LIN SAT in the operations center at the edge of Sichuan province listening to his latest orders. Ru Quan was specific and deliberate. Daiyu Lin didn't have to wonder why he was being given the honor of stopping the trespassers; he and his team were the best trained in the world. American or Russian operatives having the audacity to cross the Tibetan border without the permission of the Chinese government was a slight that would not go unpunished.

"You understand your mission?" Ru Quan asked.

"Yes. Retrieve the weapon and kill any foreign operatives in the area. Am I leading a team or moving in solo?"

"This is solo, but you can use local assets to assist you, if the need arises. Even though the Americans and Russians are able to stay off the radar for now, their trespass will be scorned by the world while ours would be condemned. It is our territory, yet we must bend to the world powers."

"What kind of weapon do you believe they have?"

"If our spy satellites are correct, you will be retrieving an outdated Russian nuclear weapon on a mobile launching platform. If we can prove that the Russians were storing such a weapon in Nepal and have since moved it onto Tibetan soil, this will be considered an act of war and dealt with in ways we have anticipated for many long years."

"How do the Americans fit into this?" Lin asked.

"They got the jump on the intelligence. Their President denies having operatives in the area, but we know that to be untrue. They wouldn't pass up an opportunity to make Russia look bad and force concessions from them at the negotiating table—and they certainly wouldn't want us to have it."

"When do I leave?" Lin asked.

"Right away. I want you in Kathmandu tonight."

"Yes, sir," he said, and hung up the phone. The Americans and Russians would expect Chinese operatives, but Lin knew he was something special. Whereas they were blundering elephants in a small room, he was a silent shadow. He intended to remain utterly invisible until it was far too late for them to save themselves.

15

Bolan raised the binoculars to his eyes, then contained his surprise as he saw the men getting out of the SUV behind them. The man in charge was known to him—by reputation, though not personally. His name was Nizar Vitaly, and he was, by all accounts, little more than a savage animal dressed in the garb of the Foreign Intelligence Service. "Son of a…" he muttered, passing the binoculars to Nischal.

She raised them to her own eyes. "Is that…?"

"Yeah, Vitaly," Bolan said. "So, they've sent their best."

"Who's Vitaly?" Solomon asked, training the glasses on the men below, then gasping as the big Russian pulled his sidearm and killed Feng. "Obviously, a serious man."

"Feng was nothing more than a tool Vitaly was using, were I to guess," Nischal said. "He couldn't have gotten here with enough of his own men, so he supplemented using Feng."

Bolan looked up the wash, then back at the road below. Feng's men were either dead or running, so it was only a matter of time before Vitaly turned his attention to the three of them. Or he'd simply take the nuke and leave. The odds were lousy and getting worse by the minute.

"We're going to have to make a run at them," Bolan said. "It's a Hail Mary play, but there's not much else we can do."

"Agreed," Solomon said. "Leapfrog?"

Bolan nodded sharply, then charged forward to the nearest cover point and opened fire. Behind him, Solomon advanced ahead of Bolan by a few yards, then used his own weapon to give Nischal a chance to do the same. The technique wasn't perfect, but the downward slope of the wash, the boulders and scraggly trees helped make it as effective as anything else. They laid down covering fire for each other as they moved closer to the convoy.

When he was close enough, Bolan fired two quick shots in Vitaly's direction, then ducked behind a large rock. Two of Vitaly's men jumped out at Bolan from a small stand of nearby trees. He dropped the first with a clean shot as the other landed on him full force.

They exchanged punches as they hit the ground, rolling over the jagged rocks. The Russian went for a knife and tried to shove it into Bolan's kidney from the side. Bolan rolled, twisted and grabbed his assailant's knife arm but only managed to divert the weapon toward his face. The Russian grunted as he applied more force. He outweighed Bolan by a good fifty pounds, and it took all of the Executioner's strength to hold him off.

Bolan let his body go limp suddenly, and in the moment it took for the Russian to react, he stretched his arm out, found a rock and pounded it into the man's cheek. The first strike dazed him and Bolan levered up on one elbow and hit him again, knocking him down, unconscious or dead.

He looked up to see Solomon fighting with two men and Nischal trying to intervene with a third. He moved to intercept, but the man on the ground grabbed his leg. Bolan kicked him in the temple without missing a stride and charged toward Solomon and Nischal. He brought up his Desert Eagle and shot one of the men attacking Solomon.

The distraction was all Nischal needed to draw her knife and, graceful as a ballerina, slit the throat of the man who was trying to grab her. His eyes registered surprise for a moment as he grasped at his neck and tried in vain to stop the flow of blood before sinking to his knees, then toppling over.

Solomon took care of the third man, driving his palm into his nose, jamming the hard cartilage into the sinus cavity. The man was momentarily stunned by the pain and burst of blood and Solomon grabbed his arm, twisting it so that the Russian's own knife penetrated his abdomen. An upward thrust at the end of the blow ensured that it cut into his vitals.

"Look!" Solomon yelled.

Bolan turned to see the truck pulling away with Jian Chen at the wheel.

"Damn! Where'd he come from?"

Vitaly and his men were already in their SUV, speeding after the truck. Automatic weapons' fire drove Nischal, Bolan and Solomon back into hiding.

Bolan brought up the binoculars and spotted at least

one encouraging sign—the sight of Raju disappearing over a hill, apparently unseen by either Chen or Vitaly's men. He had no doubt the boy could handle himself on this terrain and suspected he was headed for shelter in a nearby village.

"We have to regroup," Bolan said. "Do you know where we could go?"

"Yeah," Solomon said. "I've got a spot near here. Let's head out. We're going to need some more weapons before we can reclaim the truck."

VITALY HAD HIS men pull over while he consulted a map. He recognized Chen from the initial intelligence on the area. He couldn't let him get away with the nuke. He'd made a miscalculation in killing Feng so early; the survivors from his band would surely spread the news around the mountains, ensuring little assistance from the locals.

The sat phone rang. Vitaly picked up, and Li Soong was on the other end.

"Soong, I don't have time for your nonsense. If you've got something important to say, then say it."

"You are not very hospitable, but I am always a procurer of information."

"I know where the item is."

"Then perhaps you should finish obtaining it and make your way back here. Felicks Kolodoka is on his way and has every expectation that you will be here when he arrives."

"I don't answer to Kolodoka or to you."

"As you say…shall I pass on any messages?"

"Yeah, tell him to stay out of my way."

Vitaly hung up and pondered his next move. He dialed Grigori and waited for the curt answer.

"Is it finished?"

"No, but I have located it," Vitaly said. "One of the local warlords has it. We encountered some resistance, but things are well in hand. I would think within the next two days we will have it."

"You may not have that long."

"Is there a change?"

"We have intelligence that the Chinese are on the move. If I were you, I would expect a visitor."

"Just one?"

"If the rumor is correct, there is no need to send more than one. Locate this weapon, secure it and get out or don't bother coming home at all."

"Yes, sir."

Vitaly hung up the phone and contemplated his next move. He ordered his men back in pursuit of the truck and hoped that Jian Chen was as stupid as Feng.

THE TREK THROUGH the mountains was rough, and Bolan, Nischal and Nick were reaching the end of their energy. Solomon continued to lead the way, but as the sun began to sink, the old spy seemed to wane, as well. He paused at a rocky outcropping and abruptly turned around.

"Where are you going?" Bolan asked.

"We have to get back down the mountain," Solomon said.

"We just *climbed* this mountain," Bolan replied. "You said you had a safe place for us to hole up and resupply."

Solomon stared blankly at Bolan and then focused on Nischal. He smiled and ran his thumb across her cheek.

"You've always been so beautiful, dear, but those looks of yours can get you killed in the field. You should find someone and settle down. This is no life for a beautiful and smart young lady."

Bolan shot a glance at Nischal, who gave a slight shake of her head and took Nick's hand. "We've had this conversation already, Nick. Remember? It was before my first field assignment. I've been in the field for quite a while now. I'm okay."

The confusion that clouded Solomon's eyes vanished for a moment. He considered the mountain, then met Bolan's eyes.

"About a mile north of here, there's an old sanctuary with emergency supplies that should see us through, Colonel."

The moment passed and Solomon's face clouded over again. Nischal held his hand and Bolan led the way. Finally, they made it to the small temple. Carved into the side of the mountain, it would be nearly impossible to see from below. Bolan studied the artistry on the walls and wondered how long it had been there. A large fireplace sat in the center of the room with small shrines lining the walls.

Bolan got busy starting a fire with the plentiful supplies available and had the room warmed up in no time.

"He must have set this up as a fallback," Nischal said, pitching her voice low enough that only Bolan could hear her. On the other side of the room, Solomon gazed into one of the shrines, lost in thought.

Bolan nodded. "That's the way it looks to me, too. Why don't you do an inventory of the supplies and see what we've got to work with. I noticed some crates under the altar on the far wall, and if we're lucky, he's stored some food here, too. If not, I'll go hunting."

Nischal nodded and Bolan pulled out the sat phone he'd found earlier, then dialed Brognola's number from memory.

He answered on the first ring.

"Hal, I have a sit-rep for you," Bolan said, skipping the usual hellos. It was impossible to tell how long he'd have a signal or battery power.

"Striker! You damn well better have a sit-rep for me. We've been sitting here on our thumbs wondering if you made it out of that plane alive. The President's ready to send in a second team and both the Russians and the Chinese have people on the ground out there."

"Yeah, Nischal and I both made it out. The pilots weren't as lucky."

"What's the status of the plane?"

"It was destroyed on impact, but there was a lot of wreckage. We covered it up pretty well with some interesting help, but a cleaner team needs to get to it as soon as possible and do a better job than we could."

"Interesting help, Striker?"

"Do you remember an operative by the name of Nick Solomon?"

"Yeah, the guy was a legend. He was still working for MI-6 when I got my start."

"The thing is, Hal, everyone thought he was dead. But it turns out he disappeared—on purpose. He wanted to retire peacefully and has made his home in a Tibetan monastery. He's helping us to recover the weapon."

"You can tell me about it in greater detail when you're back here with that nuke."

"I had it, but we were overtaken. There are several

forces in play up here, including Nizar Vitaly and at least two regional warlords—though we saw Vitaly take one of them out of the game. At this point, it's kind of like which bully on the playground is bigger."

"Who's got the weapon right now?" Brognola asked. "Please don't say Vitaly."

"A local warlord, Jian Chen, last I saw it. Vitaly was hot on his heels, but he was outnumbered and it's all but dark now. What do you have for me?"

Brognola filled Bolan in on the players he was aware of and gave him more details about Vitaly's reputation. Bolan didn't need to be told that Vitaly was a cold killer—he'd seen it himself when he'd gunned down Feng and his men.

"My guess would be that you're going to have to contend with more than Vitaly. The Chinese are getting restless and our informants say they're sending a high-level operative of some kind into the area. Time is running out, Striker."

"I hear you. We're sheltering tonight, but we'll be back in pursuit at first light."

"One other thing. Weather reports for the region show another blizzard heading your way, and this one is going to hang around a little longer."

"Perfect," Bolan said. "Maybe it will slow them down."

"I don't care what it takes," Brognola said. "Get that damn nuke. Anything else?"

"One minor thing," Bolan said, glancing over his shoulder to ensure Solomon and Nischal were out of hearing range. "Solomon isn't himself sometimes. I'm not sure what's wrong with him, Hal—could be dementia or Alzheimer's—but he...gets confused once in a while."

There was a brief silence, then Brognola said, "Let's not worry about it right now. Take what help he can give you and make the best of it. Hell, Striker, he's an old man. My memory isn't what it used to be, either."

"Understood," Bolan said. "I'll update you again as soon as I can, but tell the President to hold that other team. I don't want any more players on the field than we've already got."

"Will do," Brognola said, then broke the connection.

Bolan tucked the phone back into his coat and returned to the interior of the temple. Nischal had managed to find food, sleeping bags, ammunition and some new weapons, too.

"This really was a fallback," Bolan said.

"I had to keep things safe," Solomon suddenly said. "The Russians can't be trusted."

It was obvious to Bolan that he wasn't referring to the current group of Russians they were dealing with. He was trapped in his mind, somewhere in the past. Bolan moved closer to Nischal.

"Well, *untrustworthy* is one way to describe Vitaly," he said quietly. "But it's not the first adjective I'd choose." He filled her in on his conversation with Brognola. Nischal frowned when he mentioned that he'd told Brognola about the old spy.

"I promised to protect his privacy," she said.

"I don't see that happening long-term, do you?" Bolan's expression was serious. "He's not safe out here."

"No, but maybe we can limit the information, find some way to help him out."

"When this is over, I'll do everything I can for him,

but first we have to get the nuke and all of us someplace safe."

"You have a plan?" she asked.

"Yeah—get the nuke back and get us all someplace
safe. The details we'll have to figure out on the fly."

"What are we going to do with Nick?"

"Take him with us and hope he's more lucid than
not."

"And if he gets worse?" she asked, glancing nervously at the old man.

"The weapon is the priority. Any other problems
we'll deal with as they come up. It's all we can do."

There was a long silence, then Nischal nodded and
moved to sit down next to Solomon and wrap a blanket
around him. He sat stonily silent, staring into the fire,
and eventually he and Nischal fell asleep. Bolan settled
in to keep first watch, wondering which stories from
his past would haunt him if he were in Solomon's place.

16

After the long flight to a city he'd rather not be visiting, Kolodoka was in no mood for games. He much preferred the luxuries of the life he'd built for himself in the United States, or even London or Moscow, to having to visit these backwater nations to keep the world from going up in a giant fireball.

His personal bodyguard, a gigantic mute man named Nesti, walked beside him. He'd found Nesti in a Siberian prison camp, and he was the only man he genuinely trusted with his life. Physically, Nesti fit his name—which meant "bear"—well, and when angered, he resembled the animal even more. He'd already been briefed on the potential dangers they faced in Kathmandu, and in spite of the big man's silent, stoic expression, Kolodoka had no doubt that he was on alert. They reached Li Soong's warehouse and paused at the entrance.

Kolodoka took a final drag off the cigarette in his hand, burning it down to the very edge of the filter, before dropping it to the ground and stepping on it as he made his way inside.

"That is an unsavory habit for a man in your exalted position," Li Soong said, his voice coming out the dark.

Kolodoka spun, trying to dismiss the distinct feeling that he was a fly caught in a surprising web. "And sneaking up on people and startling them is an unsavory habit for a man in your…unique position," he replied. "You always have to do that, don't you? You can never just wait for someone to actually reach your office and offer them a drink like a civilized man."

"Of course not. A man in my position cannot afford to waste opportunities at intrigue. There is little of it to be had here in Kathmandu…until recently, that is. Still, you are correct. There are much better games to play, and the one we are playing hardly requires such silliness. Under the circumstances, there may be no room for humor at all. A number of players are already in motion. This is not the time to sit at the side and watch."

"And what game is it you think we're playing, Soong? I didn't realize you had a vested interest in this." Kolodoka reached into his jacket pocket, removed another cigarette from the pack and lit it.

"On that account, I'm afraid you're wrong. You sent your dog in to attack and now you will not be able to undo the damage he's done. He's creating a full-scale disaster."

"What do you mean?"

"This Vitaly of yours has spent his time killing monks and torturing anyone he believes has information. He has not been making friends." Li Soong shook his head. "Worse, he is making many enemies and a lot of noise. He is as subtle as a rutting bull."

Kolodoka sighed. "I agree. This Vitaly is a disaster that needs to be controlled."

"If you wanted control, then you should never have sent him."

"*I* didn't send him," Kolodoka protested. "He wouldn't have been my choice at all for a mission like this."

"Whoever sent him, then," Soong said. "The responsible party will be seen as Russian Intelligence. What is your plan now?"

Kolodoka paced the floor, lighting another cigarette and thinking. Nesti remained still, watching the doorway and the interior of the warehouse. Kolodoka had hoped Vitaly would show at least some restraint, but now... He took two long drags and then turned back to Soong.

"Russia must be protected. No matter what."

"You mean that *you* must be protected," Soong replied.

"Of course I want to be protected, but the potential damage to my country comes first. This needs to be contained. The United States is already involved—I'm sure of it. And China is going to stick their big, overreactive fingers in at any minute, too. We can't start a war out here because a bunch of field assets went crazy."

Li Soong nodded. "You are correct. My sources tell me that there are already Americans in the field and that China is sending someone. Yet you are also forgetting another issue—once Vitaly has his prize, he may or may not return it to Russia."

"You think he would sell it?"

Li Soong laughed. "I think he would sell his own mother for a liter of good vodka if that was what he desired at the moment. He's involved in the market already, so if the opportunity presents itself, I expect him to…investigate."

"You know this."

"I have helped him do business in the past along with his friend Fedar."

Kolodoka paused, watching Soong with suspicion. The man was always such a shrewd character and unwilling to give information without taking his pound of flesh. Kolodoka considered his options. With Vitaly on a rampage, they were few, and none of them were particularly appealing.

"Why would you just give me this information? Why not extract a price?"

"There is always a price, but these men are bad for business. Many people will look this way if they are here killing. I prefer it when my business goes unnoticed and unexamined. There is profit in it for me to get rid of them."

"So you're suggesting we get rid of Vitaly?"

Li Soong laughed softly. "I am not suggesting *we* do anything. I am suggesting that *you* have a problem that is drawing a lot of attention. You would be wise to end the problem. Once the Chinese learn of the threats to the monasteries, there will be immediate and dire consequences."

"The Chinese don't even like Tibet."

"Yes, but in their view, Tibet belongs to them, to disparage or destroy or not as they see fit. For anyone else to do these things would be taken as a great insult."

Kolodoka nodded. "I have other things I need to see to, but you and I will meet again."

"I am always your humble servant."

VITALY SMILED AS he scanned the landscape ahead. Chen had trapped himself far more neatly than the Russian had expected by driving into a box canyon with no way out. As Vitaly's men took up positions, the gunfire from Chen's forces slowly dwindled from staccato bursts to individual shots that were easy to distinguish as they neared the end of their ammunition. Vitaly had only to wait the warlord out.

He gestured for one of his men to come closer. "Take the sniper rifle up there," he said, gesturing to the top of the ridge that overlooked the canyon. "If you see a way to clean out a few in hiding, go ahead, but keep your eyes open for my signal."

The man nodded, slung the rifle onto his back and began climbing. Vitaly estimated it would take about an hour to reach the top, but the wait would be worth it.

"This should put an end to it," Fedar said. "He can't have that many men left."

Vitaly nodded. "It shouldn't be long now."

They waited patiently for the sniper to summit the ridge, holding the other men back from advancing.

"Just fire enough to keep their heads down for now," Fedar ordered them. "There's no reason to waste lives or bullets."

Once the sniper had settled in, he immediately began wreaking havoc. He fired multiple times in rapid succession, and judging by the shouting and screaming, he'd been spotted the enemy's primary nest and was taking out the last of the holdouts.

Vitaly watched as Chen revealed himself on top of the platform that carried the nuke. In one hand, he held a grenade. As Vitaly closed the distance between them, he pulled the pin.

"Stay back!" Chen shouted. "Or we'll all go to hell together!"

Vitaly stopped with Fedar at his shoulder. "There's no need for this, Chen," he said, holding up his hands to show they were empty.

Chen's eyes narrowed suspiciously.

"You're out of men, out of ammo and trapped, and still I approach you without a weapon in my hand. We can still make a deal, in spite of your actions."

"A trick," the man said. "You don't want to die."

"You're right," Vitaly said. "I don't want to die, but neither do you. Come down from there and we'll work this out."

"How?" Chen asked. "You just want me out of the way."

Vitaly shrugged. "Sure I do, but only because I'm like you. You only want a profit—the same as I do. Come down here and we'll work out a deal that will make us both happy."

The warlord hesitated, but Vitaly could see him running through the options in his head. This was really his last chance. Finally, he nodded and slipped off of the platform. He moved cautiously toward him, still holding the grenade in one fist.

"What's the deal?" he asked.

The last of Chen's men huddled by a jumble of boulders, having thrown down their weapons and given up a fight they couldn't win. All of them held their hands high in surrender.

"Despite your treachery, I'm going to make you the deal of a lifetime," Vitaly said. "Come. Let's discuss it like civilized men."

Chen stood directly in front of Vitaly. "You understand that I… This was a once in a lifetime opportunity."

"Of course," Vitaly said. "Anyone would do the same in your position."

"They would?"

"Certainly," he replied. "Here you are, scratching out a living in the middle of nowhere, trying to get by on the slim pickings along the Friendship Highway, and then you get your hands on something worth…well, millions maybe. Who could blame you for wanting a better life? Not me, that is for sure."

"I am glad you understand," Chen said.

"He's very understanding," Fedar said. "It's one of his trademarks."

Chen took one last step and Vitaly held up a hand to stop him from coming any closer. "You're still holding that grenade, Chen," he said calmly.

Chen's head exploded as the sniper saw the signal and took him out. The shock caused the man to throw his arms up in the air and release his hold on the grenade. The lever popped off the side and Vitaly reached forward, snagging it out of the air.

He silently counted off two more seconds, then tossed it into the midst of Chen's remaining men. Fedar joined him as they tucked in next to the mobile platform and covered their ears to block out the worst of the blast.

He got to his feet, then looked to Fedar. "Finish off any survivors."

"Shouldn't take long," Fedar quipped as he stepped away.

Vitaly returned to their vehicle and picked up his satellite phone. He dialed Grigori's direct line.

"Give me good news."

"It's done." Vitaly said. "We have the weapon and we're cleaning up now. Everything is well in hand."

"That is good news," Grigori said. "I'll leave for the airport immediately."

Vitaly paused. "I'm not sure I understand. The airport?"

"I will be meeting you in Kathmandu," his boss replied. "I want to ensure that the last phase of this operation is completed without any additional problems."

"There is no need to come yourself," Vitaly protested, thinking of money lost if Grigori showed up here.

"A good superior spends time in the field as well as the office. I want to see this for myself. Have no fear, Vitaly—all will be well."

Vitaly had the sinking feeling that all was *not* well, but he had the weapon. Perhaps the time had come to do something about Grigori and ensure his own future at the same time. After all, a good superior was often promoted from within.

He put the phone back in the truck and shook his head as snowflakes began to swirl down. Peering toward the mountains, he cursed softly. A storm was coming, a big one by the looks of it, and they wouldn't be getting very much farther down the road today.

Soong watched the man strut in and knew he had a new customer. New customers were always good—they brought business and were often an acceptable alternative to current customers. Usually, they had information that would be useful in one of his many enterprises.

"May I help you?"

"I was told that you are the man with information."

"I have many talents and gaining information is one of them…for a price, of course."

"I don't give payment until I know that someone has what I need."

"I would say you are looking for some troublesome Russians and perhaps some Americans?" Soong suggested. He knew he had to be careful now. This was the operative the Chinese had sent, and Kolodoka had paid him well.

The man pulled out a wad of money and passed it to Soong. "Where?" he said.

Soong picked up the money and counted it quickly. It was hardly enough to buy a few precious sentences, whereas Kolodoka would keep him paid for years. "There is a border crossing on the Friendship Highway. I should think you would want to position yourself there."

"Why there?"

"With so many people seeking a prize in such a remote area, there is bound to be a winner and a loser. The only place they can gain a reward for their prize is to return it to Kathmandu. There is no safety in any other direction, only hiding, and none of the parties involved are interested in spending the winter in the Himalayas. They will come through that crossing."

"If you're lying," the Chinese man said softly, "you will not like the result."

"There is no need for threats. I am a purveyor of information. You paid and bought information, which I have given you freely. In fact…" Soong considered his next move carefully. "Allow me to send some of my own men with you. The Friendship Highway is no place to go alone."

"So your men can kill me and steal it once it's in my possession."

Li Soong laughed. "I do not trade in things that bring so much attention. I want my region of the world to be peaceful again. I do not care who ends up with the item, so long as they leave. My men will not harm you in any way."

Soong waved at his second, who stepped forward and bowed at the waist. "Take four men and help this gentleman acquire the object he seeks at the border crossing. Provide whatever assistance is necessary to his enterprise and do not harm him."

"Of course, sir," the man said, bowing again. He turned toward Lin and said, "If you'll follow me?"

The customer shot him a sharp, final gaze, then nodded and left the warehouse.

Li Soong watched them go, then smiled to himself as he returned to his private office. His collection was coming along nicely, and with all his new friends, he would be adding to it very soon.

17

The sun rose, and the confused old man who had huddled next to a shrine the night before was now strong and vibrant, ready to take on their opponents single-handed. Solomon moved with alacrity, and his voice was clear and sharp. Bolan watched as he and Nischal gathered up their belongings and resupplied themselves from Solomon's hidden stash.

Whatever was going on with the old spy's health seemed to get worse as the day wore on, which meant the earlier they set out, the more time they'd have him at his best.

Once they were packed, they hiked through the snow from the previous night and slowly made their way back to the long, stony wash that led to the road where they'd last seen Vitaly and the missile.

Nischal studied what remained of the tracks on the ground. "They got out before the storm hit," she said. "It would've slowed them eventually, but still, they could be in Nyalam by now."

Bolan scanned the empty landscape. "I was count-ing on some of Feng or Chen's vehicles to be here still. It's a long hike back to Kathmandu."

"Oh, you needn't worry about that, mate," Nick said cheerfully. "Another storm would come along and kill us long before we reached Kathmandu."

"Perfect," Bolan replied, but stopped before he could elaborate. The sound of an out-of-tune engine was echo-ing through the mountains and getting closer.

"Take cover," he ordered, moving back into the wash.

They'd stocked up on ammunition at the temple, but Bolan had hoped they wouldn't have to cut into their supplies quite so soon. If it was Vitaly or Chen—or any of the other warlords in the region—they wouldn't have a choice.

The truck wasn't in view yet, but suddenly Solomon stepped out of cover. "What in the hell are you doing?" Bolan yelled.

"Getting ready to hitch a ride. I'd know that truck anywhere," he shouted in reply. "Come on out."

The vehicle rounded the curve in a cloud of dust as Bolan and Nischal climbed down. The beat-up rust bucket rocked to a stop right next to Solomon. As Bolan advanced, he saw Raju peering over the steering wheel, grinning like a loon.

"Where did you come from?" Solomon asked jo-vially, leaning into the truck. "And how can you see over the dash?"

"From the monastery," Raju explained. "It was a long walk back after those men took the big truck. But I had to help!" His voice was fierce.

Bolan was relieved that the boy was safe, especially because he was responsible for putting him in danger.

He would have preferred Raju stay put at the monastery, but now that he was here, Bolan couldn't deny that the boy had gotten them out of a bad situation.

"You're a good kid, Raju," Bolan said. "Now why don't you take a break and let me drive?"

Raju slid over, then they all climbed into the truck and set off after the weapon.

"Raju, what's been happening at the monastery?" Solomon asked.

"The big man, the Russian, came with his men. They killed many and hurt more. They also took or destroyed your supplies." The boy looked down sadly. "There was no one there to stop them."

Solomon sighed. "I'm sorry, Raju."

"You mean the stash of weapons in the cave?" Bolan asked.

"Yes," the boy answered.

"Well, now we know how Vitaly's thugs are so well-armed," Bolan said, trying to contain his ire. "Have you heard anything else?"

Raju nodded. "The Russian trapped Chen last night in a canyon to the north. He killed him and all his men, then took the big missile."

"How do you know?" Nischal asked.

"There are no secrets for those who live in Tibet. We only have secrets from outsiders. It's safer that way. Well, it used to be."

"It still is," Nischal said. "Goodness speaks in a whisper, but evil shouts." She turned to Bolan and Solomon. "So now what? We don't have the firepower to take him on directly."

"We're going to have to get creative and hope the storm held him up," Bolan said. "Solomon, is there a place we could set up an ambush? Maybe something a little farther out of the mountains. We've seen how well retaking it out here has worked."

Solomon was thoughtful. "Yes, yes, there's a place near Nyalam that would funnel them into the perfect position, but we'll have to change our route to get ahead of them. It's a good thing Chen led him north. The terrain is rough, but it's our only shot at getting there ahead of him and setting up in time."

"Anything else?" Bolan asked.

"You're going to have to drive faster."

BROGNOLA POURED HIMSELF a glass of water, took a sip, then waited for Quan to enter the Cabinet Room. As the man walked through the door, his perpetual sneer did little for Brognola's mood.

"Welcome again, Mr. Quan," he said. "Thank you for coming."

"Your President is not meeting with us?" he asked.

"He'll be along shortly, but I thought perhaps you and I should have a talk first."

Quan circled the table and pulled out a chair, then slid into it. "I don't see how anything you can say to me is relevant to the discussion. You're just the toady with a clever title who has the ear of the President."

"And what's your clever title, Mr. Quan?" Brognola returned. "I ask unofficially, of course."

Quan's eyes flashed. "Your lies are unofficial, but the President's lies are not. And as you know, I am but a humble diplomat in service to the People's Republic of China."

"I see," Brognola said. "Diplomat, is it? So far, you're doing a bang-up job."

The door opened behind Quan, startling him into standing.

"Keep your seat, Mr. Quan," the President said, waving toward the chair.

Brognoia tried not to laugh as irritation splashed across Quan's face.

"Has Mr. Brognola explained everything, then?"

"No, sir," Brognola replied before Quan could respond. "This…diplomat preferred to hear the information from you."

The President leaned back in his seat. "This is an unusual situation, Mr. Quan. Normally, I don't have time to meet with lower-ranking diplomats, but since you're the man China sent, you're the one I'll talk to."

Quan played it smart and stayed silent.

"What we've discovered is much of what you've already surmised about the situation," the President continued. "There appears to have been a skirmish in the warehouse district of Kathmandu and an old Russian storage facility of some kind was compromised."

Quan waited, the silence permeating the room.

"Do you have any other information, Mr. President?"

"I'm afraid not, Mr. Quan. That's what we've got at the moment, but I'm sure you have resources in the area looking into this matter, as well." He sent the diplomat a piercing gaze. "I'm sure everyone in that part of the world is very concerned, since who knows what those tricky Russians were storing practically on Tibet's doorstep…"

"I assure you, Mr. President, that our resources in the area have been properly engaged in discovering the truth of this situation. So you are telling me that you have no...*resources* of your own in the area? No troops?"

The President sighed. "Mr. Quan, as we discussed before, such measures on our part would bring about serious international repercussions and might well violate any number of treaties or at least goodwill agreements. We have intelligence sources in the area, of course, but troops?" He shook his head. "Troops would be out of the question."

"Thank you, Mr. President," Quan said, then pushed back from the table, stood and made his way to the door. Then he paused and turned back. "One last question, if I may?"

"Fire away," the President said.

"Given what you've said, may we assume that anyone found conducting operations in Tibet that were not authorized by my government can be considered a threat to our security?"

"Mr. Quan, I wouldn't presume to tell you how to deal with unauthorized personnel within your own borders," the President said.

"You would not wish us to contact your government with this information or have your government negotiate on their behalf?" Quan asked.

The President got to his feet. Most of the conversation had gone exactly as they'd planned it, and this was the final play.

"Mr. Quan, you've implied that I'm a liar more than once since we started talking, and you've said it outright when I wasn't in the room. Don't bother to deny it, since it's all been recorded." He leaned forward. "Tell your government that you're coming home—today—and for them to send someone else. You're not welcome in my country anymore and the next person they send better be more respectful."

Quan's eyes widened as he realized what had just happened. It was possible that he'd be forced to resign in disgrace, and that was probably the best outcome he could hope for. Still, Brognola had to give the man credit for keeping a straight face.

"It shall be as you say, Mr. President," he said. "Any outsiders we find will be dealt with in our own way." He swallowed. "And I will be on a plane to Beijing before the day is out."

"Very wise, Mr. Quan," the President replied. "The Secret Service agent outside the door will escort you to the exit."

Quan spun on his heel and left.

After a minute, the President turned to Brognola. "That went well. But are you sure it will buy Striker some time?"

Brognola nodded. "I hope so. The Chinese are very serious about protocol and Quan broke about a dozen rules in his last visits. If nothing else, it might limit how much attention they'll pay to what's going on over there because they'll be busy cleaning house. Anyone or anything he's touched will be investigated—including this current fiasco."

"Then let's hope Striker gets the job done in time. If the Chinese catch him, there won't be a damn thing we can do for him."

"That's a risk he's aware of, sir," Brognola said. "It's just part of the job, so we didn't give them anything they didn't already have."

"It's a dark time we live in, Hal," the President said.

Brognola nodded, his thoughts far away. Hopefully, Bolan would do what he always did and find a way to win.

18

Solomon guided them onto a road that was little more than a rock-strewn goat path up the steep side of a mountain. As Bolan drove, he could see where a possible pass opened up high above, but the truck was struggling mightily to make the climb. "Are you sure this is the way?" he asked. "It's not looking very promising." As if to emphasize his point, they hit a large hole in the road and the whole vehicle screeched in protest.

"This is my alternate route out," the old man said. "I check it at least once a month to make sure the road is clear of any major obstacles." He looked at the sky, then quickly added, "And just because the damn snow is moving in again doesn't mean it won't work. We'll get through."

"What if this turns into a full-scale blizzard?" Nischal asked.

Solomon shrugged. "That's a risk we run anywhere out here. You know that. We need to take our chances and keep moving forward. It's our only shot at getting ahead of that nuke."

Nischal was quiet for a moment, and Bolan glanced over to see her biting her lip, as if deciding whether to speak or not. "Nick, what made you decide to steal it in the first place?" she finally asked.

Solomon sighed. "I'm tired of my home being used as a pawn for the superpowers. No one really cares about Tibet. They only care about their political agenda. Every bloody idiot with a cause leeches onto Tibet like it's a symbol made just for them. A nuclear strike launched into China would give the rest of the world something else to worry about besides trying to burn down monasteries or calling the monks who live in them criminals—or worse."

"They'd know the nuke was launched from here," Bolan said. "You don't think there would be repercussions?"

"Not if they found out it was a crazy retired operative. They wouldn't care. China would use it as an excuse and all the attention would be on the United States and the Russians. Tibet would only be a footnote."

"You were really planning on launching a nuke and killing thousands of people?" Nischal asked.

Bolan glanced at the old spy in the rearview mirror. He was staring out the window and running his thumb over his opposite hand and massaging the palm. Bolan could tell that he was at war with himself.

"I don't know, but I wanted Tibet to have a choice, a real chance. We all need to be able to make our own choices and Tibet doesn't have any at all. No matter which way we look, all we see are people who want to use us for a cause or strip us of our rights." He shook his head. "Alina, sometimes when all the choices are gone and all that's left is the wreckage of what was or what could have been, you just try to make something— anything—happen. So I did."

The group fell into silence as snow began to blanket the road. Bolan downshifted, trying to stay out of the snowbanks as best as possible and hoping he wouldn't hit anything that would disable the vehicle. Hiking out of this mountain pass would be unpleasant at best.

VITALY TRACKED AROUND a curve, his jeep almost running into the back of the truck carrying the weapon. Cursing, he floored his brakes, then jumped out of the jeep and stalked to the driver's door. The first gentle snowflakes had turned into beaded pellets, and they hit him full force. He stood on the running board and tried to shield his eyes from the weather.

"Why are you stopped?" he snarled.

"We can barely see the road, sir," the driver said. "It's not safe to continue."

"Do you see that stone wall on your left?"

"Yes, sir."

"Then keep those damn rocks on your left and push forward. I don't care if this is the storm of the century."

"Yes, sir!"

Vitaly jumped down, stalked back to the jeep and slammed the door shut.

"Fedar, if they stop again, you're going to shoot the driver and take over. I want out of this godforsaken wasteland."

"I agree," Fedar said mildly. "But I'd rather not die trying. If we have to stop, then let's stop. The storm will pass."

Vitaly turned cold eyes on his man. "Is that your final word on the subject, Fedar?"

Fedar saw the expression on his face and shook his head. "Not at all. Consider it a friendly suggestion. There's no money in dying."

"There's no money at all if we don't get to Kathmandu before Grigori shows up and takes over," Vitaly snarled. "So just do it my way."

"Yes, sir," Fedar said. "You're the boss."

THE FRIENDSHIP HIGHWAY had a distinctly unfriendly feel to it as Daiyu Lin moved into position with the men Li Soong had sent to tag along. The glimpses of the barren hillsides through the blowing snow left little room for doubt that Kathmandu was a beacon of civilization compared to the rough country of Tibet and the mountains that both protected and isolated it.

Lin watched the GPS carefully as he approached the coordinates he wanted, then slowed as he spotted the small road that would hide him until it was time to spring the ambush. He pulled off and his small convoy followed behind him.

He got out of his own truck, then waited until the other men joined him. "Get everything in place now, before this storm makes it impossible," he told them, taking in the bleak landscape. "Once it's done, move the vehicles away from the road and take shelter on the far side."

Li Soong's man nodded and ordered the others to get started but paused for a moment. "And while we take shelter, what will you do?"

"Wait," Lin said. "Wait and watch."

"For what?" he scoffed. "No one will be out in this mess. They'd be crazy."

"Not crazy," Lin replied quietly. "Desperate. Now get to work."

THE LIGHTS FROM the taxiing jet moved down the runway, the white outline of the plane barely visible through the snow. Kolodoka sat in his limo, rolling the ice in his glass and silently debating whether he'd have another drink before his comrade arrived. He decided to wait. The jet moved into the hangar and the steps dropped open. Anisim Grigori, the head of Russian Intelligence, was a complicated man, but he was smart enough to know that serious trouble was brewing in Kathmandu. He'd decided to come himself to see that things were properly resolved, and when word reached Kolodoka of his impending arrival, the spy couldn't help but take advantage of the situation.

He opened the limousine door and stepped out, raising an empty glass in mock salute.

Grigori didn't move for a long moment. Kolodoka wondered if perhaps he thought he would be shot on the spot. Interesting, especially because he'd considered it himself, but watching him squirm was so much better than having him killed. Finally, Grigori picked up his travel bag and moved closer.

"Felicks," he said, containing the surprise in his voice quite well. "It is good to see you, though…unexpected. I didn't know you were in Kathmandu, nor would I have expected the honor of having you personally meet me at the airport."

"The least I could do when I heard you were coming," Kolodoka said. "Shall we get out of the cold?" He didn't wait for an answer but climbed back inside the sleek, black car and waited as Grigori followed.

Once the door was shut, Kolodoka poured himself another drink, then offered one to Grigori. "This is excellent vodka," he said. "As sons of Russia, we are brothers of a sort. I promise you that this is more than drinkable."

Grigori took the offered drink, watching Kolodoka carefully, then nervously swallowed the liquid. Kolodoka knew the quality of the liquor would be somewhat wasted on a cretin like the man across from him.

"Where are we going, Felicks?"

"My hotel," he said. "It's the only half-decent place to stay in the whole city. I've arranged for a suite for you."

"I see. Can you tell me why I am being so honored?" Grigori asked.

"You may ask, but before I answer, allow me to ask you a question. Did you really think that letting your dog off his leash would not attract attention?"

"I'm not sure what you mean."

"I'm very certain that you do, Grigori. You may not have the exact details yet, but I'm sure your imagination can conjure what Vitaly might have done in a backwater nation like this."

The car turned a corner and slowly made its way into town.

Grigori finished the glass and then poured another. "I'm the head of Russian Intelligence, Felicks, but I can't be held accountable for the actions of every man in the agency. Am I to be held responsible for Vitaly?"

"Not if you're not here," he replied calmly.

"What do you mean?"

"I mean, tomorrow morning, first thing, you get back

on your plane and go to Moscow and you wait until I have this situation handled."

"But I have…things to take care of here. I won't accept responsibility for—"

"You'll accept whatever responsibility I make sure you have, Grigori. The only question is how much of the muck I fling in your direction."

Grigori was silent, considering his words. "If I leave, you'll handle everything?"

"Anything and everything that might have required your interference," he said. "Vitaly is an animal—little more than a rabid wolf—and worse, he's more corrupt than you are." Kolodoka took a sip of his vodka. "The smart move for you, and for Russia, is for your plane to leave at first light. You go back to Moscow and forget you ever knew the man's name. He will be remaining in Kathmandu."

"If he disappears here, there will be questions."

Kolodoka laughed. "There won't even be whispers, Grigori. He'd hardly be the first man to come to Kathmandu and never leave. Besides, there are more players in this game than you know. You've let your agency get sloppy, and if you don't clean it up, someone else will." The warning in his words was clear.

"Let me stay—perhaps I can help. I do not want this matter between us. Let me make things right."

"Your help is not necessary, nor is it wanted." Kolodoka's smartphone beeped, and he read the message, shaking his head. He tapped on the glass partition, which the driver lowered, and whispered some soft words.

The car circled back around the city and returned

through the airport gates and into the hangar that held Grigori's plane.

"I thought we were going to your hotel," Grigori said.

"I changed my mind. I will be going to my hotel, but you're leaving tonight. Pick a new destination and go there."

"You said Moscow."

"Given the information I just received, perhaps Moscow is a little rash. Distance and time are needed, and you should take a vacation. A long one. Maybe someplace warm, like Fiji. Just pick somewhere far away."

"I don't understand," he said.

Kolodoka leaned forward, then turned his phone screen toward the other man. The message was from the main intelligence director. It read: TERMINATE ALL PARTIES WITH PREJUDICE.

"I think you understand me now, yes?" Kolodoka asked. "Get on your plane and go where you will. Send the plane back or people will come looking for it. It's time for you to disappear now, Grigori. I'm giving you more of a chance than I will Vitaly."

The driver opened the door, stepped aside and waited.

Grigori's face had paled considerably during the short ride. "What will I do now?" he asked. "Where will I go?"

"You have skills of a sort," he said. "I suggest you market them, quietly, somewhere that isn't a major world power. Make a nice little living and stay off the radar. If I hear of you again, Grigori...*I* will make you disappear."

"I see," he said. "Understood."

"I hope so, for your sake, brother," Kolodoka replied.

"The old wars are over and those who linger on the battlefield or do not adapt will be eliminated."

Kolodoka watched as the shattered man staggered back in the direction of his plane and stood by patiently as it took off. It didn't really matter where Grigori decided to go, however…the pilots would no doubt kill him before they landed anywhere.

19

For a time, the storm grew so bad, they had no choice but to stop and wait it out. Finally, the worst of it passed, and the old truck coughed and wheezed its way to the crest of the ridge as rays of sunlight glinted off the sheets of ice left over from the storm. Bolan downshifted in an attempt to control their descent. The slippery conditions made driving feel more like bobsledding, but Bolan held the truck on the road.

"What do you think the odds are that we're ahead of the Russian?" Nischal asked.

"With the way our luck has been going, I wouldn't put money in our favor," Solomon said.

They traveled for about another hour until they could see the Friendship Highway in the distance. Bolan parked and climbed out, grabbing the binoculars to scope the highway. Just as he expected, he could see Vitaly and his thugs moving down the road. The weather had obviously been less of a problem in the lower part of the valley.

"I see our target," Bolan told the others. "We'll have to hurry to intercept."

"What's that up ahead?" Nischal asked, pointing.

Bolan changed his focus from the distant highway to the mouth of the road they were on. "Five vehicles. It looks like they have the same idea that we do, but they've got a head start."

"Can you see who it is?" Solomon asked.

"No, but if I had to guess I'd say it's the Chinese."

Bolan slid the truck into gear and hit the gas.

"What are we doing?" Nischal asked. "If it is the Chinese, we can't let them know we're here."

"I'd say our being here is secondary to them getting ahold of that nuke, wouldn't you?" Bolan asked.

Nischal pursed her lips, then nodded. "At least we're coming in behind them. Let's get going before someone down there spots us."

Solomon chuckled quietly. "By the looks of things, everyone down there is pretty distracted at the moment. We may have a shot at this yet."

DAIYU LIN ORDERED the men to move into position as the convoy approached. For himself, he'd chosen a motorcycle despite the icy cold air and slippery conditions. He was willing to trade warmth for the speed and maneuverability of the bike.

The support of Soong's men was questionable at best. He didn't believe for even a minute that they wouldn't shoot him in the back once they had the cargo. In fact, he imagined that Soong, a known black market player, had given the orders personally. He would need to be careful and ensure that once he'd obtained the weapon, Soong's men were no longer part of the equation.

Lin revved the bike, the back wheel kicking up dirt as he tore out onto the road. Two of the SUVs moved in behind him, and two other motorcycles took up the rear. Lin pulled a pistol from his jacket and took the first shot at the lead truck just as it came into range. He knew he would miss, but the shot had the desired effect—the truck swerved wildly and slowed down. The vehicles behind it immediately swung wide, trying to make their way around it to intercept him. He smiled, lowering his pistol for another shot, but he didn't get the chance to pull the trigger as the truck burst into flames.

"I THINK YOU got their attention," Nischal told Bolan as the lead truck in Vitaly's convoy went up in flames.

The motorcycle closing in on the Russians teetered then righted itself, and when the two SUVs behind it squealed to a stop, the men jumped out and fired wildly at the convoy.

Two motorcycles in the Chinese convoy peeled away from the group, closing in on their battered truck.

"Let's finish this quick," Solomon said.

"Nischal, take the wheel and get me closer to that bike," Bolan said, pointing to the nearest one.

Nischal took his place as he pulled himself out the window, Desert Eagle in one hand.

When the nearest bike pulled up alongside the door, he put a fast round through the rider's head, grabbed the handlebars and jumped onto the bike less than a second later. He tossed the seizing body to the ground with one hand, then took aim at the second motorcycle. The driver ducked, narrowly missing the bullet, and managed to swerve off the road and onto a small trail that ran along the base of the mountain.

Bolan holstered his pistol and followed the bike, leaving Nischal and Solomon to deal with the others. Before heading into the valley, they'd made Raju hunker down on the floor in the backseat of the truck. They covered him with an old blanket so no one would spot him and he'd be spared the sight of the violence to come. Bolan had also given the boy the bulletproof vest he'd taken from Solomon's backup shelter the night before. Raju had protested, wanting to help in the fight, but Bolan stood firm. Raju was clever and brave, but he was still a child. Bolan wasn't about to have his blood on his hands.

Bolan steered the motorcycle over the rough terrain. The small berms that couldn't be avoided turned into jumps as he accelerated. He closed the gap between himself and the other rider and drew the Desert Eagle, firing two rounds. The first caught the driver low in the back and he arched like an angry cat. A bump in the road caused Bolan's aim to be off, and the second round caught the other bike's back tire. The motorcycle careened out of control, flipping over and then smashing into a rocky outcropping, cutting off the man's screams.

Bolan revved the motorcycle and spun around, heading back for the main road, looking for the third bike. He didn't have to wait long; the man appeared to be on his way to him, having been forced to reposition away from Vitaly's men. The rider bearing down on him wore no helmet, but a simple woolen scarf covered the lower half of his face. Still, Bolan didn't need a long look to know who he was—a Chinese operative, an assassin, really, whose name was Daiyu Lin.

They'd never met, but Lin's reputation preceded him. He was a gifted killer, which meant China fully intended for everyone involved in this mess to die.

Lin drew his own weapon and opened fire, raining bullets in his direction as Bolan sped and swerved down the road. They went past each other, much like two men on horses in a jousting tournament, trading bullets as they went.

Bolan skidded to a stuttering halt. He glanced down to check a bullet graze and saw that his leg was fine, but the round had pierced his gas tank. The bike wouldn't last much longer and Lin would be at a distinct advantage.

Lin had wasted no time and was bearing down on Bolan again. The hail of bullets began and Bolan spun the motorcycle in a tight circle, but it was no use. He jumped clear just before a stray round caught the tank and it exploded.

Bolan didn't wait for Lin to make another pass, but instead used the smoke and distraction of the explosion to leap over the wreckage of his bike and plow full-force into Lin, knocking him off his own. Both men hit the frozen ground in less than elegant form.

Bolan rolled out and away from Lin as the man began reaching for the short-stocked assault rifle he'd lost in the fall. Bolan grabbed him by the leg, yanking him off balance. The heavy Chinese military boots kicked and wavered as Lin tried to steady himself and take hold of the weapon.

Bolan rocked back on his haunches and leaped forward, knocking Lin to the ground again. The assassin rolled and spun, and a knife appeared in his hand almost like magic. Bolan moved back, and his opponent took advantage, doing a leg sweep and knocking him flat on his back.

The knife descended in a flashing arc, and Bolan

grabbed Lin's wrist, the blade millimeters from his face. The jubilant face of the man was betrayed by the sweat dripping off his brow as he pushed his weight behind the knife. Bolan twisted harder, hearing the bones crack in the wrist, but Lin kept on pushing, fighting past the pain.

"You...stupid American," he panted. "You...cannot win."

Bolan strained against the pressure as Lin pressed down even harder, the blade nicking Bolan's cheek.

"Stop fighting," Lin said between gasping breaths. "Your time is done."

Bolan found another surge of strength. He twisted beneath Lin, getting a leg free and changing the leverage point.

He twisted the man's wrist even more and the knife rotated away from his face and back toward his opponent. He could see the surprise on Lin's face as he realized it was a losing battle. He adjusted his weight to move away from the blade and Bolan didn't miss the opening.

Bolan thrust upward, rolling to pin his opponent beneath him. He pressed the blade to Lin's throat.

"Who are you?" Lin asked.

"Just a stupid American, but I *always* win." Bolan shoved the blade forward, cutting his carotid.

"Colonel!"

Bolan turned to see Nischal running toward him. "The Russians got away," she said. "Vitaly didn't even slow down much and he only lost the one truck."

"At least it didn't end up in this guy's hands," Bolan said. "That is—was—Daiyu Lin. Chinese assassin. I'm pretty sure he's the one they sent to take us all out. One less player on the field for now."

"I've heard of him," Nischal said. "But his men weren't Chinese. He had local help, and the handful that was left took off after Vitaly."

"What are you resting there for?" Solomon asked as he walked up to them, Raju trailing along behind. "We've got to keep moving. We need to get this weapon before this grows more out of control."

Bolan rose to his feet.

"What happened to you?" Solomon asked him.

"I had a little problem."

"Well, there was only one of them. Surely nothing for a man of your skills." Solomon strode back to the truck with Bolan and Nischal in his wake.

"The old man has high expectations," Bolan said. "Lin was a professional, world-renowned assassin, not some cheap street thug."

Nischal smiled. "It's good to know that you can struggle, too. I was beginning to think I was the only one with a weakness."

They looked up as the truck engine revved and started to pull away with Solomon behind the wheel. Raju waved to them from the window.

"Where the hell does he think he's going?" Bolan asked.

"To finish the job."

20

Li Soong sat in his private office with four mahogany boxes opened in front of him. Each box contained a canopic jar from an archaeological dig. Soong traced the edges of the each jar. The ancient Egyptian tradition of placing the organs in jars when the body was mummified was fascinating to Soong. Each jar was magnificently decorated; the tops were figures that represented the sons of the god Horus. He lifted out the Imsety jar and marveled at the golden inlay along the fine alabaster. The afterlife was less interesting than keeping himself in this world for as long as he could, but he liked being the only one to possess certain objects. Although many people collected canopic jars, his were unique—from a new find that would soon rock the archeological world.

The phone rang and Soong gently replaced his prize inside its chest. He was patient, making certain that the boxes were closed before he picked up the receiver. He motioned for his servants to take the boxes and scowled at them, a reminder that their lives were not as valuable as his prizes.

"Li Soong," he said. "How may I be of service?"

The background road noise on the end of the line was terrible, but Soong quickly recognized his man's voice. "Vitaly broke through the ambush. Daiyu Lin is probably dead by now."

"What happened?" he asked.

His man explained the ambush arranged by Lin and how they'd been attacked from behind by what appeared to be a small group of American mercenaries.

"Where is Vitaly now?" he asked.

"Ahead of us on the road and making all speed to Kathmandu."

"Ahh…I was hoping you would have more promising news, like he'd met his untimely end along with Lin. That would've been much easier than what we're dealing with now."

"There *was* interference from that other party. We need more men to cut him off, if you want us to intervene."

Soong looked across the table at Kolodoka, whom he'd been ignoring up to that point.

"I have a solution to the problem," he said. "I'll call you back."

He hung up the phone and stared at Kolodoka.

"What is it?" the Russian asked.

"An interesting complication. The Chinese sent Daiyu Lin to intercept Vitaly and the weapon. I gave him a handful of men to order about and to keep an eye on him. They ambushed Vitaly but were ambushed themselves by a small American force."

Kolodoka raised an eyebrow. "Does your man know who these Americans were?" he asked.

Soong shook his head. "They didn't have time to ask. It sounded like Vitaly ran right over them in the chaos, and Lin is likely dead."

"Why didn't you tell me the Chinese had an operative here?" Kolodoka asked. "I could have made some plans around that."

"I do not work just for you, Felicks. We never arranged an exclusive agreement for my services. Will you quarrel with me over this?"

The Russian shook his head. "Of course not, but if you'll excuse me, I must go and help prepare a welcome for Vitaly."

"Please call me if you need anything," Soong said. "I am at your disposal."

"A simple thing, really, would be helpful," he said.

"Oh?"

"Yes, please ask your men to back off Vitaly. He'll be heading for the warehouse, where he's expecting a convoy to be ready to leave and where the last of his men were supposed to be waiting for him. I don't want him getting any ideas about going somewhere else."

"A simple enough request, Felicks," Soong replied. "I will tell my men to back off. I don't want them getting killed in whatever it is you have planned for him. What about the Americans, whoever they are? Do you want them stopped?"

Kolodoka considered this for a moment, then shook his head. "No, tell your men to let them pass. I have a use for them, I think."

KOLODOKA BOWED AS he left Li Soong to play with whichever of his toys he wanted to admire next. It was fortunate that Lin had been killed by the Americans before he could stop Vitaly or do any additional damage to the situation. He climbed into his limo and then pulled out his phone. He needed help, and calling his own government would present more questions than answers.

"Brognola."

"Mr. Brognola, it's good to hear your voice," Kolodoka said.

"How did you get my direct number?" he demanded.

"In a world filled with so many large secrets, your phone number seems a relatively small one, doesn't it?"

"What can I do for you?" Brognola asked.

"It is something that I that can do for you. I am in Kathmandu, working on our little problem. The Chinese sent Daiyu Lin, but before he could stop Vitaly or intercept the weapon, my sources tell me he was killed by a small American force."

"An American force?" Brognola asked. "Surely your sources are mistaken."

"Let me be clear with you, Mr. Brognola, and as you are a very astute man, I have no doubt you will understand me. Yesterday, I ensured that Anisim Grigori was out of the way, and today, I will make sure that Vitaly is stopped. In order to do that, I need the help of your people in the area. I don't have enough men of my own, and those I do have are rented at best."

"I told you before, Felicks, that we are not involved."

"That's too bad. I feel like a small war may be landing in my lap and I was hoping for some allies to even the odds. There may even be an advantage in it for us both."

Brognola was silent for a minute. "I'm not saying we have anyone in the area, but I'm listening."

"If your people help me stop Vitaly, I will let them

leave with the weapon, provided it's gone within twenty-four hours."

"Why would you do that, Felicks? If we can prove that the Russians were hiding nuclear weapons in Nepal…"

Kolodoka laughed. "My friend, those are matters of diplomacy that will no doubt be hashed out in private meetings between our respective leaders, not on the world stage. The United States doesn't want a war or to do any more saber-rattling than necessary. Neither does Russia. In the end, we have no reason to *not* work together. Let us agree to help one another."

"And what do you get out of it?" Brognola asked.

Kolodoka found Brognola's directness refreshing. "Two things. The first is that I rid Russia of two very dangerous men, who placed their own wealth and ambition over the needs of my country. That, I've already accomplished."

"And the second?"

"I am a collector of bones, Mr. Brognola. This would be a very big bone to have in my closet."

Brognola laughed. "All right. This is what I can tell you. If we had people in the area, I can assure you that their number one mission would be to recover the weapon at all costs. If we had people in the area, they would be very thorough."

"I admire those traits," Kolodoka replied. "If those people were in the area, is there a way you could reach them with a message?"

"Hypothetically, if we had people in the area, I could probably get word to them," he said. "What would I tell them?"

"You would tell them to come to the warehouse

where the weapon was first stolen. Vitaly will be there soon and all of this can be ended. Perhaps even a few lives will be saved."

"If I could get word to them, I'd be sure to pass that along," Brognola replied. "If we had any people in the area."

"If," Kolodoka said. "Oh, there is one other matter I might bring to your attention."

"What's that?"

"The plane you have on standby in Delhi? The one to transport the weapon, should your hypothetical team be successful in securing it?"

Kolodoka could almost hear Brognola's teeth grinding. "If there were such a plane, what about it?"

"Get it en route," he said. "Your people will need it if they're going to make that deadline."

VITALY WATCHED HIS enemies gaining on them in the side view mirror. The highway should have given them an easier time than the mountains, but the smoother terrain was giving their pursuers an advantage, too. Something had to be done to slow them down.

He pulled the truck over and barked orders. Fedar and several men jumped out, quickly wiring Claymore mines with pressure switches along the road. They climbed back into the truck and the small convoy started out once more.

An old truck careened around the corner behind them, closing the gap rapidly as he kept his pace slow. He could have gone faster but wanted to see his own handiwork. From what he could tell, two groups were involved in trying to stop him and had instead ended up fighting each other. The mines would finish them all off. In an hour or so, he'd be back at the warehouse and, shortly after that, on his way to retirement.

"Are we no longer in a hurry, sir?" Fedar asked.

"Fedar, one should always take the time to ensure that his work achieves the desired results."

In the mirror, he saw that the truck's driver was an old man. His expression was fiercely joyful as he closed in on his prey. No doubt, this was the man who'd been hiding in the monastery. He appeared intent on exacting his revenge.

Vitaly slowed even more, relishing the sense of anticipation in his gut. He smiled to himself. Despite all the little setbacks, things were beginning to look up.

The old man's gaze suddenly turned to horror as he realized he must be driving into a trap. Vitaly saw his surprise as the first Claymore exploded beside the truck. It rocked sideways, causing the other pressure plates to engage.

Stopping completely, the Russian watched as the truck spun and came to a stop, a burning hulk of metal. The flames and smoke quickly obscured the cab. Whoever the old man had been, he was dead now, along with anyone else in the truck.

Vitaly laughed and shifted back into gear, rapidly gaining speed. Now there was nothing standing between him and the warehouse.

21

Bolan barely heard the chime of the satellite phone in his pocket as he guided Lin's motorcycle down the road. Nischal clung on behind him, her arms wrapped tightly around his waist. He looked away from the road long enough to tell her to take the phone out of his jacket pocket and answer it.

"Hello?" she said. "Brognola? You're going to have to speak up. I can barely hear you!" She was practically shouting into the phone, and Bolan realized he was going to have to stop and take the call. He pulled over as she told Brognola to hold on.

"This isn't really a great time," he said by way of greeting. "I'm sort of in the middle of chasing down a nuclear weapon."

He listened as Brognola outlined Kolodoka's plan. "It's a good notion," he finally said. "But do we have any reason to trust him?"

"No, but I think he's playing this one straight, Striker. And at this point, it might be our only solution."

Bolan scanned the empty landscape around them. It had taken him the better part of an hour to get the motorcycle running again, cribbing parts from the wreckage of the other two. Nick was nowhere to be seen, and by now, Vitaly's lead was probably insurmountable without help. "Agreed," he said. "Let Kolodoka know we're coming, and get that plane here."

"It's already in the air," Brognola said. "Stay safe and let's do this as quietly as we can."

"Understood." Bolan broke the connection and quickly brought Nischal up to speed, then restarted the bike and took off down the road toward Kathmandu.

Twenty minutes later, they rounded a curve and Bolan almost laid the bike down trying to avoid the still-smoldering debris of the truck.

Before he'd even come to a complete stop, Nischal was off the back and running toward it, shouting the old spy's name.

Bolan approached more cautiously, but he could tell what had happened. The damage was from multiple Claymores impacting the truck at virtually the same time. Given the positioning of the fuel tanks on the side, it hadn't taken much to cause a pretty big fire.

"Come help me!" Nischal yelled as she tried to get into what was left of the cab.

He jogged toward her and yanked on the door handle, forcing it open.

Bolan prepared for the worst, then caught his breath as he saw the inside of the cab. There was no sign of either Solomon or Raju.

"I don't understand," Nischal said, running a hand through her hair. "Where are they? What happened to them?"

Bolan shook his head. "Let's hope they got out of the truck in time and found a place to hide. They'd still be here if Vitaly got to them."

Nischal let out a small sob. "But Raju…"

"He's gotten out of bad scrapes before," Bolan assured her. "Plus, this is his home. He knows the area and the people. If he got away, he'll be fine." Neither of them stated the obvious—that Solomon, with his deteriorating mental health and who knew what kind of injuries, didn't stand much of a chance out here, even if he survived Vitaly's death trap.

Nischal nodded, composing herself, and followed Bolan back to the bike.

"Vitaly has a lot to answer for," she said. "So very much to answer for."

"He'll get his due," Bolan said. "I promise you that."

VITALY GUIDED THE mobile platform into the warehouse parking lot, his small convoy following along. He was halfway out of the vehicle when he realized that the men on duty were not, in fact, his men at all. They wore a mishmash of uniforms, but all of them were armed and moving quickly to surround the platform.

He jumped back into the cab, cursing. "Out the other side," he snarled at Fedar. "Right now!"

Fedar quickly opened his door and guided their other trucks into position, providing cover for Vitaly and his remaining men. Behind them, another truck pulled into the gap in the fence, blocking the exit.

Without breaking cover, Vitaly yelled, "Who's in command?"

"Oh, you surely know me, Nizar Vitaly, as I most certainly know you," a deep, almost jovial voice replied from somewhere on the other side of the platform. "You can surrender now, and I will give you a merciful ending."

Vitaly laughed as he dredged the voice from memory. "Felicks Kolodoka," he called. "I heard you were retired in America, living the life of a diplomat."

"I was, until your actions and those of your superior forced my hand. Surrender, Vitaly. It's not too late to at least save some of your men."

"The Russian Master of Spies and Keeper of Secrets," he replied. "You know I can't do that, and you know that if you send those half-trained boys in here, many will die."

"I do," Kolodoka replied. "Which is why I'm content to wait. If you will not surrender, then other steps will be taken."

Several reports rang out and the tires on the vehicles in his convoy were flattened. "Hold your fire!" Vitaly yelled to his own men, knowing that if they shot back, it would be a bloodbath. There had to be a way out of this mess, and what he needed was time.

"Excellently done, Felicks," he called out. "I cannot surrender and I cannot leave, but you cannot come and get me without creating a scene too big for you to cover up for Mother Russia. A standoff, yes?"

"I quite agree," the man replied. "But there is one difference between us."

"What's that?"

"I have all the time in the world, and you, my friend, do not. I am content to wait."

"Then you can damn well wait!" Vitaly snarled.

He turned his attention to Fedar, whose expression,

for once, was less than serene. "If you have any ideas," he said, "now would be a good time for one."

Fedar shrugged. "Nothing useful comes to mind at the moment, sir, except to die with honor."

"You're a fool, Fedar," Vitaly said. "What makes you think there's anything honorable left in this world?"

BOLAN GUIDED THE motorcycle into Kathmandu, avoiding the main streets and numerous market squares, and followed Nischal's directions to the warehouse. She was familiar with the city and had studied the location of the warehouse on their flight over. He could see the mobile platform and Vitaly's small convoy surrounded inside the fence line. The gate was blocked with another truck, but there was enough room for them to slip inside.

He brought the bike to a stop as he saw the stalemate in play before him. Something or someone had to give or there was going to be a very big mess to explain to the world. This couldn't be kept quiet if it turned into a big gun battle. A fairly large man waved in his direction from his position behind a large, black limousine.

"I expect that's our host," he said to Nischal.

"It is," she replied. "That's Felicks Kolodoka."

"I'm still surprised he came out here," Bolan replied as they walked toward the man. "He was supposed to be retired."

"Do we ever really retire?" she asked, obviously thinking of Solomon.

"I don't suppose we do," he admitted.

They reached the Russian and Bolan nodded in greeting. "I understand we have you to thank for Vitaly's welcome party."

He shrugged modestly. "And you are the Americans

who aren't actually here," he replied. "You're a very solid-looking pair for a hypothetical."

"I get that a lot," Bolan said. "So, is Vitaly pinned down behind the platform?"

"All business," Kolodoka said, nodding his approval. "Yes, he is, but he's in like a tick. Getting him out without losing a lot of men will be difficult."

"I see that," Bolan replied.

"Was there an old man or a child with him?" Nischal asked intently.

Kolodoka shook his head. "I'm afraid not. I'd heard you were a party of at least three or four."

"We got separated just south of the border," Bolan said, studying the situation. "Do you have any ideas on how you'd like to play this out?"

Kolodoka nodded. "Yes, I'm going to get back in my car and have a drink. While I'm there, I suggest you kill Vitaly. The rest of his men will surrender after that."

"Sounds simple enough," Bolan said. "Just saunter over and take him out."

"I'm sure you'll think of something," the Russian replied. "I did my part in locking him down until you could arrive. The rest, as they say, is up to you." Then he heeded his own words and climbed into the back of the limousine.

Bolan turned to Nischal. "I've got an idea."

"What do you have in mind?"

"I'm going to call him out," he said. "I think I can get him to play, but you can't get involved. I need you to watch my back because he's going to have someone watching his."

"I can do that," she said. "Just try not to get yourself killed."

"I'll do my best," he said. "Stay on my six, but give me enough room to maneuver if he comes out."

She nodded, following along in his wake as he moved into the open area between Kolodoka's men and Vitaly's convoy. "Hey, Vitaly!" Bolan yelled. "You don't have a reputation for being much of a hider. Why don't you come out here and we can settle this like men?"

"And get shot for my trouble?" Vitaly yelled in reply. "No, thank you. Though I've been wondering when the Americans would show up. You've been a thorn in my side since I got here."

"I've done what I could to make your life miserable," he said, "but you've stayed ahead of me until now. And left quite a path of bodies behind you."

"People got in my way," Vitaly said. "Some had to be persuaded to part with information. That's what we do in our business, my friend."

"No," Bolan said. "That's what *you* do, you coward."

"I'm no coward!" Vitaly yelled, genuine anger in his voice.

"Fine," Bolan said, "Then prove it. Come out and fight. Just you and me. If you win, you and your men walk. You won't get the nuke, but you'll be alive."

There was a moment of hushed conversation, and then Vitaly appeared around the front of the mobile platform. "Do I know you?" he asked. "What is your name?"

"Colonel Brandon Stone," Bolan replied. "But I'm not officially here, any more than you are. We're both off the books, and Kolodoka isn't watching, so what do you say? Care to make a go of it?"

Another man appeared beside Vitaly, whispering

rapid words into his ear. "Shut up, Fedar," the big man said. "We don't know who this man really is."

"You don't, and I left my identification in my other pants at home."

"If I beat you, my men and I walk out of here?" Vitaly asked. "No weapons, just man to man?"

Bolan nodded and turned to Nischal. "Get Kolodoka out here."

She jogged to the car and opened the door, quickly explaining the offer to the Russian. Kolodoka appeared long enough to give the orders, as Nischal returned to stand behind Bolan.

"I don't see any better choices," Vitaly admitted, "and I like killing Americans." He put his guns on the ground, took off his coat and started to move forward with his man at his back.

"Then come get some," Bolan said, dropping his own weapons and moving to meet him, trusting Nischal to watch the other man carefully.

From the outset, it was obvious that Vitaly had been trained in Sambo, the mixed martial art form from Russia, whereas Bolan's training had been much more varied. They were a near match in reach, but Bolan had speed. Elbows, hands and knees all engaged at once as the two men clashed and grappled, each seeking an opening to take the killing blow that would end the fight.

Vitaly managed to get in close, and Bolan had to ram his knee into his ribs to break out of the Russian's hold. He needed to do the unexpected, and that meant going to the ground, where he wouldn't have the advantage of speed.

Bolan faked a stumble on the uneven pavement and Vitaly grinned, surging forward as Bolan fell.

As they hit the ground, Bolan snapped his legs up, wrapping Vitaly's throat in a choke hold with his knees and using his own body weight against him. Grunting, the Russian tried to escape, twisting and turning, but all of the force went directly into Bolan's already braced shoulders.

As he tightened his grip, preparing to finish it, he saw Fedar make his move out of the corner of his eye.

The underhanded throw was almost perfect, and the slim blade of the stiletto moved too quickly for Nischal to see until it was embedded in the back of Bolan's thigh. With a cry of rage, Nischal took a run at Fedar. Bolan grunted in pain, his hold on Vitaly loosening. The Russian broke free, grabbing Bolan's ankle and twisting it painfully before jumping clear.

"Now we'll fight," he snarled as Bolan rolled to his feet.

The Executioner could feel the blood dripping down the back of his leg and knew that he had to finish this quickly or his own end would be at the hands of this Russian animal. Dying in a warehouse parking lot in Kathmandu was not what he'd had in mind when he'd started this mission.

He braced himself for the Russian's next attack.

22

Nischal saw Fedar throw the knife, but there was nothing she could do to intercept it. Instead, she charged at the man, surprising him with the ferocity of her attack. Like his boss, Fedar had trained in Sambo, which involved a lot of locks and grappling moves. Nischal, however, had trained in two forms: tai chi and aikido. She flowed like water, eluding his grasp and delivering stinging countermoves that soon had him infuriated.

"Hold still, woman," he said, rushing her. She stepped away once more and turned, but a crack in the pavement tripped her up. He was on her in a second, his arms wrapped around her throat in a choke hold that would render her unconscious in very short order—if he didn't just break her neck instead.

She flailed against him, but he was much stronger. Nischal began to see stars and clawed at his arms, trying to get even the smallest breath of air. She felt a pang of sorrow that she'd let the Colonel down, that Solomon and Raju were probably dead somewhere.

"Just relax," Fedar whispered into her ear. "It will be over in a second."

"Like hell it will, mate," a voice said from behind them.

Fedar released her to face this new attacker but had barely turned when Solomon drove the blade up between his ribs, twisting it ferociously. Fedar spasmed once, twice, then died and Solomon dropped his lifeless body to the pavement.

Nischal gasped for air. "Nick!" she said, running to him. "You're alive."

"Of course I'm alive," he said. "Just waiting for my moment. Plus it took me a while to get here. This is bad country for hitchhiking. I ended up in the back of a truck with some goats."

"What about Raju?"

"I sent him off to the nearest village. Too many close calls. He's a good kid, brave and loyal, but I wasn't about to let him get killed on our behalf. As much as he was trying to."

She hugged him quickly, grateful for his aid and his presence and relieved about the boy. Then she turned to watch Colonel Stone face off with Vitaly. Both men were bloodied and battered.

"Stone, stop playing around with that stupid Russian and kill him already," Solomon called. "It's cold out and I want to get inside."

BOLAN HAD BEEN able to keep Vitaly off long enough to see that Solomon had somehow appeared out of nowhere and managed to save Nischal's life. Now it was just Vitaly and him. "Let's get this over with," he said. "I'd hate to keep this going after sundown."

Vitaly seemed shaken by Fedar's sudden death but nodded. "With pleasure."

They closed on each other once more, but this time, Bolan didn't bother to grapple with the man at all. Solomon was right—it was time to stop playing around. He allowed Vitaly to wrap him in a bear hug, then swung his arms wide, clapping his hands down as hard as he could on the Russian's ears. He almost felt the popping sensation as his eardrum's ruptured.

Vitaly released Bolan, staggering backward, dizzy and unbalanced. Pressing his advantage, Bolan slipped to one side, locking up the Russian's swinging right arm, then driving the elbow sharply down, breaking the arm and causing Vitaly to bellow in agony.

Bolan stepped behind him, wrapping him in a hold very similar to the one Fedar had applied to Nischal but with one difference. Vitaly thrashed, trying to break free, but Bolan wasn't concerned with how much or how little oxygen he had in his lungs.

Bolan twisted, canting his left hand in one direction and pulling with his right in the other. Vitaly's neck snapped, the sound alarmingly loud in the silence that followed.

"Better," Solomon said in approval. "Much better. Another decade or so in the field and we'll make a real fighter out of you yet."

Exhausted, Bolan staggered away from the body. On the other side of the convoy, the last of Vitaly's men threw down their weapons in surrender.

Kolodoka reappeared, directing his men to the right places.

"You fight very well, for a man who isn't even here," he told Bolan.

"Thank you," the Executioner said. "You should see me in person."

Nischal and Solomon crowded in then, and Kolodoka drifted away, a giant of a man following in his wake.

"Are you all right?" Nischal asked.

"He's fine," Solomon said. "He'll be right as rain in the morning, and then we're off."

"Off?" she asked. "Off where?"

"Someone's got to deal with these Russians on their own turf, plus there's a mess of trouble in some of the other Slavic nations. I'm sure that's where they'll send us next."

Nischal and Bolan exchanged a glance. Once again, with the sun going down, the old man had lost his grip on the present day. Nischal's face was sad with the knowledge that the man she loved like a father wasn't the same man he'd always been.

"I'll get him situated in a hotel, and then once it's dark, we'll move the platform," she said, pitching her voice so that only Bolan could hear her.

"Fine," he said. "I'll stay here and keep an eye on things and get myself cleaned up."

"Come on, Nick," Nischal said, taking the old man's arm. "Let's go get settled in for the night."

Bolan watched as she led him away. Even now, with his mind disappearing, Solomon's skills were sharp. It was a shame to see him deteriorate.

NISCHAL GUIDED THE heavy mobile platform through the gates and into the street. They were following a lead SUV, provided by Kolodoka, for the short drive to the airport. Bolan didn't feel much like talking and, apparently, neither did she.

Twenty minutes later, the SUV pulled onto a side road next to the airport and Bolan saw the jet waiting for them. Nischal drove up to it and climbed down from the cab. The SUV would take them back to their hotel.

The Air Force officers that met them nodded solemnly at them. "Try to be careful with it," she said as she looked at the vehicle, which was pockmarked with bullets and covered with mud and ice and gravel. "We've babied her all over the place."

The officer laughed and signaled for his men to load it aboard the aircraft, and they watched in silence until it was done. "Want to wait until it's airborne?" she asked.

"Oh, yeah," Bolan said. "I'm not leaving until it's gone and totally out of my hands."

"Agreed."

They waited some more, sitting in the back of the dark SUV, until the flight took off.

"It's over," she said. "We did it."

"I suppose so," he said.

"So what's next?"

"A shower and a shave," he said wryly. "And then, who knows? Unfortunately, stopping one war usually just means another one is brewing somewhere else. I'll go where I'm needed when the time comes."

Nischal nodded, then smiled sadly. "You know, even though the mission's done, I still feel like I've lost an important battle."

"What's that?"

"Nick. He's just…he's not himself anymore, and I doubt he ever will be again, at least not for longer than a few hours a day. I feel like I've failed him. Maybe we pushed him too hard…"

"Nischal," Bolan said, meeting her eyes. "You can't

blame yourself. Nick was a damn good operative—one of the best—and I'll never forget everything he did for us on this mission. It's a shame, what's happening to him. But we can't change it. No one can."

"Still," Nischal said, her tone resolute. "I'd like to stay here with him, make sure he's all right. He taught me so much, it's the least I can do."

Bolan couldn't argue. He'd been wrong about Alina Nischal—she had more than held her own on this mission, and he knew she hadn't even tapped into her full potential as a field agent yet. But she had to do what she believed was right. And Solomon would be safer, more comfortable, with someone like Nischal looking after him.

"Well, the show's over," he said. "Might as well head back to the hotel."

Nischal agreed and Bolan tapped the driver. As the buildings of Kathmandu sped by, Bolan reflected on Solomon's condition, thankful that his own mind was intact. He'd seen a lot over the years, things he sometimes wished he could forget. But it was the memories—good and bad—that kept him going, made him more determined than ever to keep fighting. This mission, Solomon, Nischal…after tonight, they'd be memories, too. And tomorrow, he'd find out where he'd be making new ones.

* * * * *